BUCKET LIST OF SORTS

Leah Battaglio

A Bucket List of Sorts is a work of fiction. Names, characters, places and incidents are the products of the author's imagination or are used fictitiously. Any resemblance to actual events, locales or persons, living or dead, is complete and utter coincidence.

Copyright © 2020 by Leah Battaglio
www.leahbattaglio.com

All rights reserved.
No part of this book may be reproduced in any form by any means without express written permission of the author.

For Barbara K.

Chapter 1

As I sat in the hot, stuffy office of Whitaker, Leeves and Munchin, I sipped my bitter "office coffee" and thought about my last visit here. Mr. Leeves was the attorney who attended to my late husband's estate needs. I say 'late' because a few years ago my husband Steve of seven years died in an automobile accident while away at a real estate conference. Only, he wasn't at a real estate conference. A late evening phone call from a hospital in Napa Valley proved that. My husband died alongside a woman in the car they rented to travel around wine country. Another driver hit them as they returned to their Bed & Breakfast from a day of wine tasting. One shouldn't jump to conclusions but unfortunately, I knew this was all rather suspect since his real estate conference was supposed to be in Denver.

As a result of my husband's unexpected death, I was a widow with two small children and piles of accounts I never knew existed. Thankfully, Steve was a saver and wise investor. He also, thankfully, had a little black book in his desk with the username and passwords of his secret life's accounts. Everyone in the law office knew the backstory by the time we settled the estate. It was hard to keep it a secret, however they were all very professional.

There was a previous visit to Whitaker, Leeves and Munchin a few years before Steve's death, as well. It wasn't a shocking death; it was however just as painful. My Great-Aunt Beebie lived a long life. When she passed at the age of 85, nobody was surprised. Her health had been failing for several years. The flame that once glowed intensely gently faded until it was nothing but a slow flickering candle. Watching my dear aunt transform into a person I barely recognized was agonizing to the point that some days it was difficult to breathe. Despite the pain, I visited Aunt Beebie as much as I could and held her hand until her very last breath. While those memories are painful to recall, I have a million memories of the wonderful times. Those are the memories I hold close to my heart.

My Aunt Beebie was one of my favorite people in the entire world. As a child, I would spend long weekends with her at her house on the hill. She never had children, although she tended to her garden, pets and me as though we were just as special. We would go on long walks in the woods looking for fairies. I was convinced the dragonflies were simply disguises for fairy princesses wandering through the forest looking for magical flowers. Aunt Beebie agreed and we would go back to her house to discuss this while I painted her face with Avon makeup to give her a movie star makeover. Although she probably looked more Drag Queen than Beauty Queen, my aunt never balked. She was kind, patient and always treated me like a person rather than a silly kid.

"Thank you for your patience," said a tall, aging

man in a pinstriped suit as he burst into the room with an arm full of papers. "I realize this is rather strange for you, given the fact your loved one has been gone for some time now." He set the papers on his desk, put on his glasses and proceeded to shuffle and re-stack his pile papers and envelopes.

Why was I here? What loved one was he talking about? Why doesn't he turn on that fan sitting in the corner of the room? Why did I forget to put on deodorant this morning?

"I'm afraid Mr. Leeves, you'll have to be more specific. The estates for both of my loved ones have been finalized for years. I don't understand why I've been called here, to be honest."

The attorney's face fell somewhat as he realized who I was. The woman whose husband died with his mistress. Yep. That was me.

"Ah, Mrs..."

"Nope. Gonna stop you right there. I am Ms. Loxley. Tilda Loxley. I went back to my maiden name after all that, well, you know. Don't worry, I had a conversation with the kids since their last name is still Marlowe. Yes, it was confusing at first and then every year there is confusion at school because they still want to call me Mrs. Marlowe. In retrospect, perhaps I should not have done it, but I cannot take another trip to the social security office and DMV to change it back even if I wanted to. Besides, after finding out he cheated on me and then went and died before..." I suddenly felt a drip of armpit sweat down my arm and hoped the commercials weren't true about stress sweat.

As I rambled on, Mr. Leeves looked at me, expressionless, then interrupted me to say, "Of course, Ms. Loxley. My apologies. Let's get started, shall we?" Mr. Leeves relaxed a bit as he put the papers down in a tidy manner and folded his hands under his chin. "This is in regard to your Great-Aunt Barbara Loxley."

"Aunt Beebie? Is something wrong? I received everything in her will years ago. Was it a mistake? I have the books, but the money is long gone. I used it to buy a fancy television that turns into a picture frame when I'm not using it. And a new washer and dryer! I knew I shouldn't have splurged on the fancy front load option and custom color. Who needs a navy-blue washer and dryer?? Who needs an art television? My TV is always on. What was I thinking?" My head started to feel warm and my hands were beginning to tingle as I realized I may be asked to pay back money I was not prepared to return. I was five seconds from a mild panic attack.

Mr. Leeves seemed to know what I was thinking. "Ms. Loxley, no, no you don't have to pay any money back." He may have been ten seconds from a panic attack as well. "Grace, please bring a bottle of cold water in for my client. Grace?"

The elderly assistant rushed in as fast as an elderly assistant can rush in and gave me a pre-opened bottle of very cold spring water. She patted my shoulder and asked if there was anything else, she could do, which of course she couldn't because

I already died of humiliation.

"As I was saying, your Great-Aunt had a clause in her Last Will and Testament. She left instructions for us to present this envelope to you on your 40th birthday. I apologize, we are a few weeks off since your birthday was earlier in the month. The electronic reminder had a malfunction, Grace left herself a note just in case and well, here we are. Would you like to open it now?" His face perked up with excitement and Grace lingered in anticipation. Like me, they were quite interested in this mysterious envelope. As much as I wanted to leave and make my own discovery in solitude, I didn't want another reason to come back here with more questions.

I carefully opened the manila envelope to find a smaller envelope, with my name on it. I knew the handwriting immediately. Aunt Beebie had the most beautiful handwriting. It was from an era where penmanship was appreciated, and typing was a luxury.

I took a deep breath and read the letter to myself, much to the dismay of the elder attorney and Grace.

My dearest Tilda,

I hope you are well. I'm sorry I missed your birthday. Being dead has some disappointments and that is just one of them. As you know, I had many adventures in my youth. I traveled alone to the Far East, got arrested for protesting the war, published books of my photography, just to name a few. That being said, I find myself sitting in this old chair, looking out my window seeing life pass by. I still have things I'd like to do. Places I'd like to see. There never is enough time to live it all, is there? In response to my sudden need for more, I have concocted a plan. I may not be able to fulfil my destiny, but you can. Go live Tilda. You will find a list of the things I would like you to do for me, a bucket list of sorts. I have also ensured you will have plenty of funds to fulfill my requests. Sweet girl, did you honestly think I would only leave you a bunch of books and pocket change? You were my world in the living and will be in the afterlife. I will always be here for you, Tilda.

All my love,
Aunt Beebie

I sat in shock desperately holding in my tears. As I read her words, I could hear Aunt Beebie's voice as though she was sitting right next to me, whispering in my ear. I skimmed the list of things she had left for me to accomplish, not really absorbing any of it. I noticed Mr. Leeves fidgeting in his chair, not wanting to be rude, but anxious for me to tell him the meaning of it all.

"So, it appears my aunt has a bucket list she would like me to finish. She also mentions funds to compete this mission?"

"Yes. We have a trust set up in your name. She has left you a considerable amount of money. Did you know your aunt was so wealthy?"

"What do you mean, wealthy?" I asked. I knew she did well for herself but was conservative when it came to spending money on certain items. She always said, *Why, on earth buy lettuce when I can grow it myself?*

The attorney smiled and provided me with the exact dollar amount. My sweet, lettuce growing Aunt Beebie left me approximately $2.8 million dollars and her bucket list to spend it on.

Chapter 2

I would have preferred to get in my car and drive to Target, for an overpriced coffee and wander aimlessly until I figured out how to process the recent turn of events. Unfortunately, this mom had a Parent Teacher Association board meeting to attend.

When someone mentions PTA, the images of uptight, loud, opinionated cliquey women may come to mind. These stereotypes have been perpetuated by movies, sitcoms and memes. I'd like to say being a PTA parent is just the opposite; a group of women coming together to achieve a goal of making the school a better place for the children. Unfortunately, I am sorry to say it is not. At least the PTA at my school, Jean Bradley Patten Elementary. I will say some ladies are nice. A few women who I can walk past in the hall and know they will smile and greet me. They won't talk about me behind my back or intentionally try to make me feel as though I don't fit in or belong. I thank the heavens for those ladies every day because if not for them I would have gone to dark places in order to cope with TABITHA.

SHE walks the halls as though she owns them. With her perky blonde ponytail and weird color sports drink, Tabitha Wells chats with teachers and waves to other parents like a proud PTA President should. For some reason however, she treats me like I'm the girl who stole her boyfriend at the prom. Even though we are adults, this is not high school, and I've barely spoken to a man unless he fixes my plumbing or rings me up at the grocery store checkout. To be clear, that wasn't a euphemism or innuendo. I haven't been on date since my husband died but that doesn't matter to Tabitha Wells. It's possible she doesn't even know I'm a widow. That's how little interest she has in knowing me. Despite my being a part of her PTA.

We recently completed a huge Back to School fundraiser and thankfully only have a couple of Spirit Nights, where we eat at certain restaurants and then in turn that restaurant donates proceeds back to our school. I typically do a quick to-go order for that one. We also have the exciting and somewhat frenetic Book Fair that is held in our school library. It requires volunteering and helping our sweet librarian collect money and keep the books organized. I avoid that as much as possible because, the tight quarters of a library filled with people and chaos pushes my mild anxiety to the limit. Our PTA also has the Thanksgiving Food Drive and *Be Kind We Don't Mind Week* where each day a certain theme requires fun and creative dress to promote kindness and wellness. Our grand finale for the first half of the year is the Winter Party in which we under no circumstances mention Christmas so as not to offend anyone. It's all very politically correct these days.

All of this is far from my mind because visions

of luxurious pedicures are dancing through my head until a gentle nudge to my arm woke me up to the realization that everyone is staring at me.

"Welcome back, Tilda." Tabitha Wells said, staring at me with her 'what the fuck' expression. "Do you have this month's PTA membership total? Last year we were already at 500 PTA members. Mindy, you were such a Rockstar. Are we near that yet, Til?"

Shit. I totally forgot to look that up before our PTA meeting. I mean, I forgot deodorant, was I really going to remember this stuff?

"One sec. I think I have the program on my phone." I scrambled through my purse, pulling out reusable grocery bags, receipts, granola bars and Play-Doh? What was that doing in here?

"It's fine Tilda," Tabitha said, while typing carefully and quickly on her super slim, totally high-tech laptop that she always has with her. "Okay got it."

"Found it!" I said. "Now, let me see..."

"Tilda, I already have the numbers. 372. Since it's October 31st, it looks like we've missed out on this month's goal again since we are about a hundred members short. No worries, it's fine Tilda. I know you're doing your best." Tabitha gave me her fake smile as the secretary diligently jotted down her notes for the minutes. I couldn't help but wonder if she would include our President's tactful public shaming of me.

We moved on with the rest of the meeting and once it finished, I couldn't wait to get to my car. Part of me wanted to sneak a peek at my kids for my own comfort but it is highly frowned upon to disrupt class time. Volunteers are to be invisible. So, home I went to finally discover my fate according to Aunt Beebie.

Home is my comfort zone. There are many days I would be perfectly happy to not leave it. School drop offs and walking the dog do not count since I can successfully complete those tasks without talking to anyone but my kids or George, our Beagle mix. She listens to me and rarely judges, unless I'm trying to make some sort of excuse why I can't possibly feed her dinner at 3pm. Yes, George is a girl dog with a boy name. It sounded cute at the time but now I spend most of my time telling vet techs, dog groomers and everyone else that she's not a boy. Despite the flower collar and pink leash.

"Hi George! You won't believe my morning. Treat?" I dip my hand into the crystal jar of dog treats and grant her wish.

"It's now or never, George. I'm going to open the envelope. Am I nervous? Noooo. Ok, there's no bullshitting you is there? Yes, I'm a bit nervous." George, who had little idea what I was rambling on about, just sat there waiting for more food.

I prepared a cup of coffee and sat down. I wasn't sure if it was the unknown that scared me or the idea that my life was about to change. My normal, which to be honest isn't that exciting would now be about trying new things and stepping out of my narrow comfort zone. I didn't know if I was prepared, or even capable.

"All right, George. Here we go." I open the envelope and unfold the piece of paper. The shaky but familiar handwriting lists twelve adventures.

Fly in a hot air balloon
Kiss a stranger with reckless abandon
Learn a new language
Take a gondola ride in Venice
Sleep overnight in a haunted house
Run a long-distance race
Sing in front of an audience
Learn to dance
Pose nude for an art class
See the Northern Lights
Take a road trip anywhere
Teach a class

While some things were doable such as the road trip anywhere or maybe learn a new language, others seemed nearly impossible. There was no way I would be nude in front a room full of strangers! I don't even like to be nude in my own bedroom. Run a long-distance race?! When I ran down the street once chasing after George, who came loose from her leash in a hot pursuit of a squirrel, I successfully peed my pants (thanks childbirth) and nearly had a heart attack. Exercise has not been a priority the past few years.

As I tried to subdue my rush of panic, I received a phone call from Mr. Leeves, the attorney who was handling all this craziness.

"Ah hello, Ms. Loxley. I'm sorry to bother you but I forgot one last request of your aunt."

Not sure I could handle any further surprises, I let out a deep breath and said, "Go ahead Mr. Leeves. Lay it on me."

"Very well. It appears the late Ms. Loxley has asked that you complete your mission in a year. She fears you will procrastinate and not finish it without an err, kick in the butt is how she explained it here."

"A year?" I couldn't breathe. How in the hell was I supposed to take care of my kids, my life and do all the things she couldn't do in her entire life in a year?

"Or what?" I asked Mr. Leeves, somewhat defiantly.

"I'm sorry?"

"Or what? What happens, Mr. Leeves if I don't complete it in a year?"

"Your aunt has a response for that. One moment." Mr. Leeves hummed as he presumably scanned his documents. "Oh, here it is. Ahem. She says if you do not finish the list in a year, she will be disappointed in you."

Oh, Aunt Beebie. She knew me so well. I didn't need punishment. A simple disappointment was enough. It always was. My parents never put me in a corner or gave spankings, which is what most parents did back then. They merely furrowed their brows, tilted their heads with a slow nod and told me how disappointed they were with my behavior. I would cry and internally berate myself. Maybe the spanking would have been easier.

"Yes. Oh and Ms. Loxley, I have arranged everything with the bank for the transfer of ownership to the funds. You are now on the account and the recipient of $2.8 million, give or take some fees. Is there anything else I can assist you with? "

"No, I don't suppose there is unless you know how to clone me a few times with that million dollars?"

Mr. Leeves laughed uncomfortably and replied, "I'm sorry no. Goodbye, Ms. Loxley."

"Goodbye, Mr. Leeves."

I suddenly felt very alone.

Admittedly, I don't have a lot of friends. When I got married and had Logan, who is ten and then Livia six, I dedicated most of my free time to them. Once they were enrolled in school, I went back to editing, but freelance. It gave me a lot more flexibility and I didn't have to drive into an office every morning. It also meant my social interaction was mostly limited to coffee baristas, who might learn my name but forget it by the end of the order. I do have one good friend though and thankfully she lives in my neighborhood.

Cassie Cooke and I met while attending a school function when our kids were in the same preschool. Neither of us were really interested in the other mom groups, but we had the same sense of humor and interests (coffee, wine and Bravo Reality TV), so our friendship was a good fit from the beginning.

One of the few things we don't have in common however, is her presence on the PTA. Cassie is all for donating but has zero interest in being on a board. I sometimes feel the same way however, I committed to it for a year, and the kids seem to like me showing up at school occasionally so I don't think I can get out of it anytime soon.

"George, are you ready to go pick up Logan and Livia from school?" Sometimes, when I don't get a chance to take George out for a proper walk, we go on car adventures. George likes to ride in the car and gets excited when she sees the kids. Even if it's simply sitting in a car pick up line waiting for the kids to run out of the school.

My sweet dog lifts her head at the kids' names and jumps off the sofa in anticipation of her trip.

I load George in the car, and we make the 1.27-mile journey to the carpool line at Patten Elementary. And then we sit. And sit for about 20 minutes.

"Oh, there they are, George!"

Logan and Livia hop into the car and greet George first, naturally.

"Did you guys have a good day?" I ask as Logan fights the dog off from her multiple kisses.

Logan groans, "Mom, I got my folder signed today for talking too much."

"Your folder signed? So, what do you have to

do?"

"Nothing. I just need to talk less, and you need to sign my folder saying you know I got in trouble."

Wonderful.

"Okay, Logan. But you need to listen to your teacher instead of what your friends have to say. It's disrespectful."

"Okay," he said, rolling his eyes. I suppose it could be worse.

"I had a great day, mommy!" Livia interjects. "We watched Mary Poppins in music today!"

"That sounds fun, Livia! I'm glad you had a good day!"

We had a busy evening scheduled since it was Halloween. Cassie and I planned on meeting up for Trick or Treating with our kids which makes it extra fun. Once I got the kids home, I fed them some spaghetti marinara then helped them get dressed into their costumes. Logan finally decided on the astronaut costume while Livia chose to be a doctor with a Princess wig for good measure.

"Mommy, this wig is itchy." Livia complained as we walked down the street the meet up with Cassie and her twins, Jameson and Michael. I was happy we had this Trick or Treating date so I could fill her in on my utterly bananas day.

"Wait, so she waited like eight years to give you this list? Why?" Cassie adjusted her son's flashlight headband while he tried to run down the street with the other crazed children.

"Well, she wanted to wait until my 40th birthday." I handed her the list to review and ease my mind of the impossibility of it all.

"Oh my god. Tilda!! How did you let me forget your 40th birthday? I'm so sorry!" Cassie is a good friend who occasionally forgets things. I don't think it's due to early onset dementia or lack of caring. I think it's more being a busy mom of identical twin boys and a wife to a husband who travels practically all month for his job.

"It's fine." To be honest, I didn't want to celebrate turning 40. I wasn't excited about it and would have preferred to forget about it all. Thanks Aunt Beebie.

"Oh, it isn't fine. I have three different calendar reminders and I still can't remember my best friend's birthday. I'll get a sitter for us and we'll go out tomorrow. I can bring the boys over to play. Michael don't push! They are smaller than you!!!" Cassie reprimanded Twin One and got back to the list. "Tilda!!!! This is amazing!" Then she started laughing hysterically.

"I gather you got to the one where I have to be naked."

"I'm sorry. I shouldn't laugh but you have the highest aversion to nudity of anyone I know, which I don't understand because you have an adorable body. Also, the trips to Venice and the Northern Lights sound like wonderful adventures but can you afford it? I can't imagine trips like that are cheap."

"Well, I actually have that covered. Aunt Beebie left me some money. A few million dollars in fact." It was difficult to actually say it out loud. Never in my wildest dreams would I have imagined that much money just sitting in a trust account for me.

Cassie stopped walking and stared at me. "Are you serious? Tilda. You're a millionaire? Are you going to move away? I know this isn't about me, but please don't move away. You're the only person in this neighborhood I like." She said, squinting from the tartness of the sour patch candy she "borrowed" from Twin Two's bag, who wouldn't notice. Sour candy was on the lower end of the boys' sugary treat favorites list.

"I'm not moving away. In fact, I don't want anyone else to know about this and would prefer to keep my life as is. Well, I might go shopping at a store that I don't also buy my milk from, but apart from that, I really don't want this to affect life for me and the kids."

"Slow down Jameson!!" Cassie shouted to Twin Two. "Good idea. I've seen on TV how a lot of lottery winners lose their minds from having millions of dollars suddenly. I have a financial lady that can help you with investments and planning. I worked with her at my old job. Jameson! Let Livia get her candy! Sorry, Tilda. I'm trying to teach them manners. I'll make them give her some extra when we get home."

Judging by the weight of Livia's bag, I think my

daughter had plenty of candy. In fact, she could barely drag it down the street.

We walked back to my house, inspected the candy for friendly neighborhood poison and razors and only let the kids have one pound of sugar, while stealing half a pound for ourselves.

As I put Livia and Logan to bed, I couldn't help but marvel at them. They had been through so much. They had no idea of the circumstances of their father's death. They were so young; it would've been inappropriate to talk about it. Logan was seven, but Livia was only three at the time. I wanted to ensure their innocence. Sure, they can be awful tyrants; complete buttheads on some days, but I don't know how I would have gotten through it without them.

"Mama, I'm not tired!" Livia whined from the bathroom as she brushed her teeth.

"Me neither!" Logan chimed in from his bedroom where I hoped he was putting his pajamas on and not getting into his toybox looking for heaven knows what. Judging by the sounds erupting from that direction, I knew the latter was probably the case.

"I want to watch a movie!" Logan yelled from what I could tell was the depths of his toy box.

"You're not watching a movie. It's 8:30. You need to go to bed!" I shouted from my bathroom as I brushed my teeth. I also needed my bed. This day had kicked my ass.

"But there's no school tomorrow! Please! Please!"

A relentless Logan shouted while entering my bedroom with his drawing pad and pens.

"Yeah, please mommy! Logan wants to watch a movie! In your bed! So does Baby Missy," Livia said walking in behind Logan with her blanket, Baby Missy and Baby Missy's blanket. And then George pranced in to stake her claim on the bed.

"Ok. We'll watch a movie. It better be appropriate, Logan. We aren't watching creepy science fiction movies...or horror movies."

They argued for about ten minutes, compromised on a creepy animated "kids" movie and fell asleep ten minutes later. I fell asleep five minutes after that.

Chapter 3

As promised, Cassie reserved her sitter for the evening so we could go out for my belated birthday celebration. The sitter came a few minutes early which helped, because I wasn't close to being ready to go out and socialize with other adults. I had no idea what to wear, my flat iron was taking forever to heat up, and I still had black hairs to pull out of my chin. I was not in a good place.

"Mama, I don't want a babysitter. I hate babysitters. They're so boring and they treat me like a baby." My oldest grumbled while I struggled to make my hair look like Jennifer Aniston's. It wasn't working, by the way.

"Logan, I need to go out and have a break. I love you. Now, go eat your pizza before the dog does." I love my dog. She's very sweet. She's also a ravenous beast who would eat your hand off if it was attached to a slice of cheese pizza.

As Logan stomped back down the stairs in ten-year-old protest, I could hear Cassie coming up.

"Tilda? Are you up here? Are you ready?" Cassie asked with a cringe as she scanned my brown, messy half-done hair and coffee stained white t-shirt.

"Oh my god, no!" I was horrified she'd even ask. "I can't stop finding hairs on my chin to pull. ALL my entire *out in public* clothes are in the dirty clothes basket. I am certain my hundred-year-old flat iron has finally retired so my hair is half smooth, half frizzy."

I looked at Cassie with desperation and said, "Maybe we should do this another time."

"Put the tweezers down. This is exactly why you need to go out. You can't have another time because this is your birthday night. What? You want to wait another year?!"

Cassie, with her authoritative purpose and tiny body marched into my closet, rifled through the multiple pieces of clothing I'd thrown on the floor in despair and put together an outfit.

"Here you go. I know you've worn something like this before." Cassie handed me a pair of slim black pants, a loose fitting sheer black top with a camisole underneath and sparkly heels.

"Spray some Febreze on the pants and let's get out of this bathroom before the steam ruins our hot mom makeup."

I composed myself, put my hair up in a simple topknot and followed Cassie downstairs with determination. I was happy to see the kids sitting at the table with their pizza and IKEA cups of water happily discussing some new YouTube channel.

"Hi! I'm Maddie. I hope it's okay I took out these dishes. I wasn't sure if they used ceramic or plastic." The tall, lanky teenager sorted all four kids out, gotten them to eat and was already preparing the pizza for the fridge.

"Mommy! Maddie knows who my favorite YouTube guy is!" Livia announced with excitement. My six-year-old is obsessed with being a YouTuber.

I don't even know how that's done but apparently people make a solid living out of it. I think I'd prefer she learn how to read and write first.

"That's so exciting, Liv! Do you guys need anything before we head out? Maddie, I've left a cheat sheet for you. Please call or text if you have any questions. I set up the air mattress upstairs if the kids want to do a camp out and watch movies. And don't forget..." As I continued to ramble on like a typical nervous mom does when she leaves her biggest joys in life to a complete stranger, Cassie interrupted, or rather, rescued me.

"I'm sure Maddie knows just what to do. She is a very responsible 16-year old. She will text you in an hour to keep you abreast on their iPad watching and running around." Cassie hugged Jameson and Michael goodbye and gave the babysitter a *text her-get-it* look while the babysitter replied with an obvious wink in return. I hugged and kissed my kids and followed Cassie out to the car. Car, or was it... no...a party bus limo?

"What is this?! I thought we were getting an Uber or something?"

"It's your birthday! I want to do it right. I called my husband's friend's brother and he gave me a good rate on a limo. Get in! We have some fun to have tonight!"

Cassie popped open the Prosecco and filled two clear plastic cups from the limousine cabinet. I had to admit, it was quite good and helped ease my nerves.

"All right, Cass. You win." I took another long sip of my drink and motioned her to top off my cup with the bubbly. If I was going to enjoy this night that my friend generously arranged for me, I needed to loosen up...a lot. I'm not a big drinker anymore, those days are far behind me since becoming a mom. One cup should do it.

We went to dinner first. I celebrated with some rather excellent blueberry margaritas. The chips and salsa were marvelous and delayed the extreme drunken behavior...For about an hour.

"Cassie! Let's go somewhere fun!" I suggested, rather loudly, as we exited the upscale Mexican restaurant.

"This place wasn't fun? I think our waiter thought you were hysterical. We probably need to do this more often." Cassie said, thanking the hostess before we left.

"Oh, it looks like Maddie sent you a text, Tilda. The kids have set up their sleeping bags. Of course, Jameson and Michael are still awake. Your kids are fast asleep."

"Yes! Let's go do some karaoke then! But first let's have a shot. Look, there's a bar over there."

Cassie jumped up and down excitedly and said, "I know where we can go!" We hopped into our limo and Cassie gave directions to our next destination.

We pulled into the older part of town and walked into a pub that was lively with people and a cute guy with a guitar at the front. Wow. Those blueberry margaritas packed a punch. They were a gift that kept on giving when combined with random shots of whatever and glasses of Prosecco. I was feeling incredibly out of sorts, wild and free... free to do whatever my heart desired.

The next thing I knew, I was waking up in an intensely dark room. It must be the middle of the night, although my bedroom, even on the darkest of nights is never typically this dark.

"What is this?" I thought out loud, feeling around my bed. My soft, organic cotton duvet felt rough, like linen and I couldn't find my bedside table lamp. I realized quickly... this was not my bed and I was not in my bedroom.

"Good morning!" A deep, coffee smelling voice proclaimed in the dark.

"AAAAAAAAGGGGGHHHHHHHH!" I screamed in horror. I had obviously been kidnapped somehow and drugged which was clearly why I had no recollection of what happened or where I was. This! This is why I don't go out and socialize!

The deep, coffee-smelling voice screamed in unison with me, then let out some expletives in an accent of some sort.

"Shit!" He pulled the curtains open and I could now see a man with coffee spilled all over him and a tray that once carried said coffee on his rug.

"Who are you? Where am I? I will not be sold to an underground pimp organization." The man moved closer towards me. "Stop right there or I'll hurt you with this." I said, as I grabbed the first thing I could off the bedside table.

"I'm not a pimp, Tilda! That's a remote by the way. The only damage you'll do with that is put on one of those Kardashian shows."

"How do you know my name? Did I tell you? Did you rifle through my things? Oh geez. Did you see all of my personal stuff?" I didn't bother to transfer necessary going out items to a reasonably sized purse last night so unfortunately, the Mary Poppins bag came along. It is always full of everything from tampons to crayons to dirty socks to Play-Doh, and so forth. It's rather embarrassing to say the least.

The coffee smelling man, I now realize is rather handsome with his 7:00 a.m. shadow. And while things are still fuzzy, I am almost certain he is not a pimp.

"Tilda, we met last night. I'm Deacon, Cassie's cousin. We met at the pub. Where I work? Brodie's?" I just stared at him blankly.

"Bloody hell. I knew you were drunk. So, you don't remember anything?" He chuckled as he cleaned up the coffee disaster that was the result of my blood curdling scream.

"Deacon. Oh my. Yes, I think I do remember, Deacon. Let me think...

He poured another cup of coffee from his carafe and sat down on the end of the bed.

"Milk?"

"Yes please."

"Sugar?" He asked with a sly grin.

"No. No sugar." I responded firmly.

"Ok let me help you with any gaps you may have."

He handed me the coffee and my hand brushed up against his. I felt a zap of electricity that must have been from the dry air. I looked up at him and saw he had beautiful, pale blue eyes and sandy, dark blonde hair that was due for a haircut. His hair stuck up all over the place in a fuzzy mess, yet it seemed to work for him. He had a deep chin dimple and small scar under his eye that made his handsome face perfectly imperfect.

"Do you remember coming to Brodie's at the end of the night? Cassie brought you there for one last bit of fun."

"That beer place with the loud music? Yes, it's coming back to me now. That's where you work?"

"It was karaoke night. You insisted on singing a Journey song. Eh, err, "Don't Stop Believin'" I think. And then you dragged me on stage to sing with you."

The haze of memories was starting to come back to me. It wasn't a smoky room, but it did smell of wine and cheap perfume, well stale beer to be precise.

"Okay this is all coming back to me. I'm confused though. Why am I here? Did we? Oh, no did we???" I was in a state of panic.

"Um no."

"Well you don't have to act all firm and haughty about it."

"Tilda, you were so drunk there's absolutely no way I would have done that. You're a lovely kisser though." His cheeky smile would have been a bit more enjoyable if I wasn't a) furious and b) embarrassed beyond belief.

"So, I was too drunk for sex, not too drunk for you to kiss me?"

"Actually, you kissed me. At the pub. On the stage. Journey has that effect on some people, I guess. I promise we didn't do anything else. Okay that's not true. We did have a passionate kiss over there on the sofa before you passed out."

I looked around the room and slowly realized where I was. Cassie had a small mother-in-law place behind her house. Cassie said it was for when her extended family came to visit. I always thought it was more for when she wanted to watch her own TV shows without interruption or judgement.

"So, you're staying in Cassie's guest house? Where are you from originally?" His accent was obviously Irish. It made me want to hear his story and basically anything that came out of his mouth.

"From outside of Dublin. I moved here a month ago. I tend bar at Brodie's and play my music a few nights a week there."

Cassie had mentioned a relative coming to stay with her a while back, although she didn't really say anything more about it. She never mentioned that it was a young, handsome, charming gentleman who says he doesn't take advantage of drunk old women.

"Well, Deacon from outside of Dublin, I'm sorry for being a hot mess and taking up your morning. I think I need to call for a ride and get out of here. My kids are probably wondering what happened to me. OH MY GOD, MY KIDS! Who's taking care of my kids? That babysitter? I've abandoned them!"

Panic and hyperventilation started to consume my body and I thought I might pass out. What kind of mother am I? I went home with some strange, much younger man with complete abandon. My children depend on me and I let them down. What if someone called the authorities? What if *they* called the authorities??

"Ssssh. It's okay, Tilda. Cassie left me to take care of you and she went to your house to stay with the kids. They're fine."

"Well, I suppose you can't be all that bad if Cassie trusts you with me. You seem like a nice boy."

"A nice boy?! How old do you think I am?" he said laughing as he poured another cup of coffee with milk and no sugar for me. "I'll have you know I turned 28 in September.

"Twenty-eight huh? That's sweet."

"Well how old are you then?"

"How rude! You never ask a lady how old she is."

"I can when she calls me a child. So, what is it then? You are friends with Cassie, and you seem to think you are years more mature than me, I'll guess... 35?"

He guessed 35 and being the sweet boy, he appeared to be, I'm sure he thought I was much older. I felt like such a pervert being attracted to a guy who was twelve years younger than me.

"Forty. I was celebrating my belated 40th birthday last night."

"And a bucket list I recall."

"I told you about my bucket list?"

"You did."

"And did I kiss you with reckless abandon?"

"I believe you did."

"I'm sorry."

"I'm not. I told you. You're a lovely kisser." When he spoke to me, he looked at me. He really looked at me. His eyes were tender and honest. While he was only 28, he seemed confident and matter of fact. I don't think my husband ever really looked at me, at least once we were married. I suppose that may have explained his affair.

Truth be told, I wanted to kiss Deacon with reckless abandon again. I didn't really remember much of the first time. It had been a very long time since anyone showed any interest in me in an actual hot chick way.

"Okay, enough of this nonsense. I need to get home."

"Oh yes, Cassie texted me and instructed me to give you these. You know, so you don't have to do the walk of shame." Deacon handed me a pair of Cassie's old sweats and a hoodie with some slip-ons. Walk of shame indeed. I hadn't performed one of those since my twenties.

"Would you like me to give you a ride?"

As much as I should have said no, I really didn't want to walk three streets over in my state. My stomach was churning angrily from my recent choices. I couldn't blame it. My choices were terribly irresponsible.

"That would be nice. Thank you."

Cassie only lives about a five-minute drive to my house. We're in the same neighborhood, although her street is at the beginning of the "higher end" houses, hence the mother-in-law cottage in her backyard. She also has a wine cellar. Our friendship was meant to be.

I changed into the clothes Cassie loaned me and Deacon led me to his car, where he held the door open for me to get in. It was clean, much cleaner than my car. No goldfish crackers hiding between seats, no sparkly glitter leftover from a random toy, or multiple water bottles on the floor. It was definitely the car of a man without children.

"So, I've sung in front of an audience and kissed a stranger with reckless abandon. I can't believe I finished two of Aunt Beebie's bucket list items and I can barely remember doing it."

"Ah, don't be too hard on yourself. There were plenty of people recording it on their phones. I'm sure you could track it down. In fact, I'm pretty sure Cass has it on her phone."

"Oh God! Seriously?! I don't want to see it! I just want to remember it. Those are two completely different things." I wanted to bury my head in Cassie's oversized sweatshirt and not come out for days.

"Well according to Google Maps we're here. Shall I walk you in?"

"God no! I sent Cassie a text. We're going with the story that I was out running early morning errands. That doesn't include picking you up!" I moaned to the far too handsome, Deacon as I dragged myself out of his car.

"Will I see you again?" He asked before I could shut the door.

"Probably not. I'm a daytime person so I don't really, um, go out at night. I have kids. So, you're a bartender and 28 and um, I'm not 28. So, no I don't think so. Thank you for the ride. Oh, and I'm sorry for, um, yeah. Okay bye!"

I took off straight to my front door before I could ramble on and embarrass myself anymore. My lonely and lustful self said, 'Absolutely!' and 'Are you kidding? Of course. You're hot as fuck and I haven't done that in a hundred years!' and just a simple 'Yes please.' I'm keeping that person to myself, though. Nobody needs to know about all that, specifically, cute, adorable Deacon from just outside of Dublin.

I wasn't sure if I was mad at Cassie for leaving me last night or thankful, because she was able to do damage control and take care of my children. However, I walked into my door with purpose and confidence.

"Hey, you made it home from your errands!" Cassie exclaimed as I walked right past her towards my downstairs bathroom. Thankfully all children were upstairs and could not see my face get greener and greener from the nausea that overcame me during my last moments with Deacon.

"I don't know if I'm happy or mad at you right now," I said to Cassie. I'll let you know after I puke."

Chapter 4

It had been a week since my successful, although somewhat humiliating experience of checking off two bucket list items. Cassie apologized profusely always adding that her young cousin was trustworthy and most definitely NOT a serial killer or pimp, as most people we meet in the world are not. She also admitted to finding Deacon scrumptious and could not possibly understand why I was not interested in dating him.

Ever since my night out, I'd been curious as to what led Aunt Beebie to want to kiss a stranger with reckless abandon. She always seemed like a free spirit. Maybe she wasn't quite as free as I thought. I think she would have approved of my choice of strangers. Deacon was so cute and despite our age difference, I couldn't stop thinking about him.

Unfortunately, I couldn't sit and daydream about my handsome stranger for long, I had a meeting scheduled this morning.

I walked into our November PTA Board Meeting as I typically do…late. The other board members were tucked into their seats, captivated by their phones and laptops. There were various levels of laughter from quiet giggles to full on roll on the floor pee your pants hysterics.

I squeezed myself into a spot next to the one mom that seemed to find the least amount of joy in whatever was happening. As I put my things down, she looked up and gasped.

"Tilda! You're here! I mean, of course you're here. Everyone, Tilda is here!"

The room got quieter as everyone put away their various devices and directed their attention to Tabitha as though to ask what they should do in this awkward moment. It was awkward because they were watching me, drunk me, but me all the same. Apparently, Tabitha Wells was at Brodie's as well.

I had chosen not to view Cassie's recording of my performance at Brodie's. My dear friend assured me it was deleted after my refusal to watch it and all that was left in the past with my foggy memory. Unfortunately, Cassie didn't realize there were other people in the audience that night, probably because she was taking care of my drunk ass. People that find it simply hysterical a fellow mom can become so drunk she makes out with a stranger onstage while trying to also sing an uplifting, joyous rock song by super band, Journey.

While I was sure the city is full of Mean Moms, there was only one who would stoop low enough to share such humiliating debauchery with the other PTA moms. The perfectly evil Tabitha Wells.

I was furious.

My head got hot and my blood started to boil. "Would the class like to share? Something appears to be SUPER funny!"

They just stared at me. Some looked fearful.

Some looked perplexed. Some stared blankly because that's what they do all the time.

"Calm down Til. We were just laughing at a viral video." Tabitha said casually as she put her phone down and stared at me.

Wait, did she say viral video? For a moment, I wondered if I was losing my mind for no reason. Now they'd really think I was a lunatic. But I was sure I heard the same Journey song I belted out that night. So, I was told anyway.

"Oh. What is it?"

"What's what, Til?" Tabitha asked, now seemingly annoyed. I hated it when she called me Til. Nobody except my husband ever called me Til. I didn't like it then either.

"The viral video, Taaaaaaabitha."

"Oh, it's just you. Singing with some barfly, attacking him on stage with your tongue. Nothing much. Can we get to business now? We have a big agenda this morning." Everyone giggled uncomfortably.

I leapt across the table and yanked her ponytail out of her head...no, not really. I wished I could do that. But no, I just sat there, shocked someone would go out of their way just to make me a joke. I was speechless.

I added my contribution regarding our sponsors and membership and said nothing else. I smiled politely at the grandmother who handles box top rewards. I nodded in agreement with the mom who felt we should start organizing the Spring

Carnival committee, without using last year's, Bounce House Bonanza Company since their service was sub-par... apparently. I waited until the meeting came to an official close and quietly exited the meeting room.

I happened to follow Tabitha Wells as we were walking to our cars. She has always intimidated me for some reason, yet today I had enough of her.

"Tabitha, I need to ask you something." I announced boldly, behind her.

She turned around, arms full of folders and shoulder bags. She looked at me and sighed. Her eyes were tired. For the first time I saw a small crease in her forehead. It was satisfying.

"What is it Tilda? I'm kind of in a hurry."

"I need to know something. Why do you dislike me so much?" There. I finally asked the question that had been on my mind forever.

"I don't know what you're talking about. I'm really busy, Tilda. I'm sorry about the video. It was funny. Okay?"

"No, it's more than that. I feel like you have a vendetta against me. You go out of your way to make me feel like shit. I just need to know. Did I do something to you?"

Tabitha put her bags in the back of her car, turned to me and said, "Tilda, do you recall Monica Jensen?"

"No. I don't think so. Is she a mom here?" Truth be told, the name sounded familiar still I had no idea who she was. I wasn't very social when it came to the other mother's here. Cassie was really the only mom I hung out with from school and she wisely chose not to be in the PTA.

"Of course, you don't. Why would you remember her? Monica Jensen was my sister. She died in a car wreck with a piece of shit guy." Her eyes were angry and tearful.

Monica Jensen. I had forgotten her name on purpose. I knew exactly who the piece of shit guy was Tabitha referred to as well. My husband, Steve.

"Your piece of shit husband was having an affair with my sister. He was filling her with all sorts of stories about how he was going to marry her one day. His mentally ill wife was so fragile though. He had to wait until the time was right. Instead he'd take her on romantic getaways where they could pretend."

"I wasn't mentally ill. I had some post-partem depression after Livia was born, but I started taking anti-depressants and going to therapy, I was fine. He told her I was mentally ill??!!"

"That's your takeaway from all of this?!"

"Sorry, no, no it isn't. I'm so sorry Tabitha. I really am. I heard your sister's name once and then blocked her out of my mind. I'd just found out my husband was dead and having an affair all in one moment. It was the worst moment of my life. I didn't know. I didn't know about any of it!" I cried out and Tabitha's face finally softened.

"Which leads me to the burning question. I

understand why you hate my husband. Why would you hate me, though? This wasn't my fault."

"I guess I didn't have him to take it out on. It's easier to be mad at someone who's right here. He was your husband. Maybe if you'd been a better wife, he wouldn't have cheated or something. Yes, I know it isn't rational but that's how I feel."

"I'm so sorry for your loss." I felt relieved to finally understand where Tabitha's animosity towards me was came from.

"I'm sorry too, Tilda. I'll take down the video, although I don't know if it will do any good. It really has gone viral. People love to laugh at moms making fools of themselves." She shrugged and got in her car. It wasn't a dig. It was the truth.

Abruptly, I took a step toward our reconciliation "Tabitha, would you like to get together one morning? For coffee or something? Maybe to talk more?"

Tabitha paused as she pulled her seatbelt over to the latch. Maybe that was the last thing my nemesis wanted. I just felt like we needed more than a quick conversation in the school parking lot to make things better for us.

"Sure. How about tomorrow morning after school drop off? I'll meet you at the new little spot by the Trader Joe's."

Still in somewhat shock, I said, "That sounds great! See you tomorrow."

Tabitha nodded and started to pull out of the parking spot, paused, popped her head out of the window and added, "Oh, and Tilda, you go girl.

That guy is H.O.T. hot. I've been eyeing him every weekend I go to Brodie's. I'm married but you aren't."

Tabitha Wells sped off in her cute little European crossover SUV, leaving me truly speechless. I'd just had a moment with my arch nemesis, and it was safe to say I was at a loss for words.

Later that day, I talked Cassie into meeting me at the Chick-Fil-A to let the kids play indoors after school on this rainy November day. I had been promising them they could go for about two weeks and since it was a Spirit Night at school, I would take care of two things at once. Make my kids happy while also contributing to our PTA.

My kids had already downed their chicken nuggets and waffle fries by the time Cassie and the boys got there. Michael and Jameson left their mother to order the same meal and ran off to join the chaos, otherwise known as the indoor play area.

Cassie sat down at our table and said, "So, you're actually having breakfast with THE Tabitha Wells? That's the craziest thing I've heard in days. I about spit out my coffee when you sent the text." Cassie said as she took a drink of her frosted lemonade.

"You should have seen me, Cass. I was so furious at those women laughing at me like they'd never seen someone's mother act that way."

Cassie waved her hand and said, "Ah, they were probably just jealous, Tilda. Most of those women have sticks permanently up their asses. I am still in shock, however, that you confronted the head bitch."

"Me too. I hate confrontation. Something just got into me. Maybe I channeled Aunt Beebie. She never would have taken any crap from any of those ladies. I still haven't told you the whole story yet."

"What? Oh my god, Tilda. There's more?" Cassie said as she dunked a piece of chicken into the sauce.

"I know why Tabitha hates me or hated me so much. I don't know, maybe she still does a little."

"Why? God Tilda get on with it!"

"Okay. So, Tabitha's sister died alongside my husband. Steve was having an affair with Tabitha's sister, Monica. As in, Tabitha's sister, Monica died alongside my husband." I finally said it out loud to someone else. Repeating the story made my stomach turn in knots.

Cassie practically choked on her chicken nuggets.

"Are you fucking kidding me? What else did she say? Did she know of the affair? Has she always known it was your husband? Is that why she's so mean? Oh my god and you're having coffee with her tomorrow? Do you need me to come?"

Cassie's anxiety about the whole thing was making me even more anxious.

"As much as I appreciate the support, I think Tabitha and I have more air to clear. She doesn't need to be my BFF, I already have you, I just think we still have things to talk about. Your questions, for instance, could be answered."

"Mama, can I have ice cream now?" Livia ran up, sweaty from her frantic chasing of boys and girls.

"Sure. I'll go order some. Please be sure and Purell your hands before you eat anything. It's flu season."

The kids enjoyed their ice cream cones while Cassie and I helped the Chick-Fil-A employee clean up our mess, which included a dumped out sauce cup, spilled ice water, dropped ice cream cone from Livia that was replaced by a kind employee and a rainforest worth of napkins.

"Okay, Tilda. I'm dying to find out how tomorrow goes. Good luck." Cassie hugged me and we headed to our respective homes to help our kids with mind boggling math questions and spelling lists galore.

The next morning, I woke up early. I didn't sleep well and wanted to have plenty of time to get ready before Logan and Livia woke up. There was no way I would look as good as Tabitha, but I could at least try.

The kids woke up early as well but thankfully late enough where I just had to finish some makeup. There was still plenty of time to make them breakfast and get them organized for the day. We were off to a good start.

"Okay guys, we need to get moving. I don't want you to be late for school." I said, putting their lunchboxes and water bottles in their backpacks.

"Where are you going? You never put real

clothes on for drop off." Logan grumbled as he looked for his other sneaker under the living room sofa.

"I'm having breakfast with someone."

"Who?" Livia asked, helping Logan find his mysterious shoe.

"A mom from school. Mrs. Wells."

"Abigail Wells' mom?" Logan asked.

"Yes, why?"

"No reason. She's nice. Abigail Wells. That's all. We're science lab partners at school. In science labs. She's just nice." Logan stumbled over his words and I couldn't help but think my little sweet boy had a crush on my (hopefully) former enemy's daughter.

"Oh, well, I'm glad she's nice. Yes, we're just having breakfast. We're on the PTA together."

With the help of his little sister, Logan found his shoe in the coat closet and we were off.

Once I got the kids to school, I drove over to the breakfast place. It was a cute little restaurant that served quality Italian coffee with healthy and not so healthy options.

Tabitha had already arrived, probably dropping her kids off minutes before the tardy bell even thought of ringing.

Tabitha took a sip of her green beverage and said, "Hi. How are you?"

"Hi! I'm good! No coffee for you?" I asked, anxiously.

"Oh no. I don't drink coffee. Never liked the

stuff. I had an early morning training session, so I like to have something nutritious after."

"Coffee for me please," I said to the young server when she came to our table. What to eat? I thought to myself. I was starving, however; I didn't want to look like a pig in front of Tabitha. Still, if I didn't eat and allowed my blood sugar to drop, maybe I'd say something wrong, or worse, honest. "Oh, and can I have some Eggs Benedict, please? Extra hollandaise on the side? With hash browns."

Tabitha just stared as I ordered. Such a disappointment I assumed.

"So, Tilda. What have you been up to? I guess I haven't really gotten to know you apart from our meetings."

"Well, I've been busy with the kids and I have a bucket list to complete."

"A bucket list?" She asked, staring blankly.

"My great aunt left it to me as part of her will. I must finish the bucket list she wasn't able to. Hence the grand display at Brodie's that night."

"Ah. Okay, so you had to make out with somebody in public?"

"No, not exactly. Well, kind of." Now that I thought about it, that pretty much was what I needed to do.

"It sounds like your aunt was pretty fun. All my aunts ever do is tell me if I'm gaining weight or need to use retinol."

"They sound like a hoot."

"Yeah, I love the holidays." Tabitha rolled her

eyes while taking another sip of her healthy green drink. Then, as though she realized something, her face dropped.

"Tabitha?"

"Sorry. Talk of the holidays brings back memories of Monica. She was so funny. It never fazed her when anybody said anything negative to her. She'd just say something witty back to them. I'm sure you don't want to hear about your husband's mistress." She apologized and I wasn't sure what to make of this different side of Tabitha Wells.

"No, it's okay. Maybe if I understand her more, I'll understand why it happened. The affair."

Tabitha let out a deep breath as she wiped the table with her napkin, "She wasn't a bad person. She wasn't perfect, but she wasn't mean. She fell in love with the wrong person."

"Did you know? I mean, I know you knew he was married. Did you know who he was married to?"

"No. I didn't know until after it…they…"

I could tell Tabitha was on the verge of a meltdown over the discussion of her sister. The waitress, who had no idea the depth of conversation, saved us.

"More coffee?" She asked me, pouring a fresh brew into my cup. I almost asked her if she had something else to pour in there, joking of course. If I drank this early in the morning, I'd probably need a nap under their table. But the air was tense, nevertheless.

"Tabitha, I'm so sorry. I feel like I judged you

based on your perfect hair and the evil looks you'd shoot at me. I didn't know the whole reason behind them." Daggers. They were more like daggers, but I didn't tell her that.

"I think I owe you a sincere apology as well. I didn't know you. I'm glad we had this today, this chat. I feel like a lot of weight has been lifted off my shoulders. Thank you, Tilda."

"No Tabitha, thank you. The weight has been equally lifted. I'm not over my husband's infidelity by any means. It helps to talk about it with you though."

We quietly finished our breakfast without any further mention of death and betrayal.

Chapter 5

The Thanksgiving break finally arrived for the kids, which, left me home with two wild children. It also gave me a break from making lunches, fighting about school appropriate outfits and seeing people.

Things were far less tense with Tabitha and me since our conversation. I dare say our relationship almost turned into something, err, friendly. I didn't see her in the same superficial way, and she could get off her chest something that I believe was eating at her soul. Who knew I could have that kind of effect on someone?

The week-long break also gave me a chance to look at my Bucket List to assess what I could accomplish soon.

"What do you guys think about a road trip? Maybe we could find a national park nearby to stay at or something."

"Can we go to roller coaster park?" Livia asked, as she slurped her cereal.

"Yeah! Let's go to that amusement park! You said we could go one day, Mama!" Logan exclaimed, choking on his pancakes.

As much as I dreaded the idea of a trip to the amusement park, their excitement at the mere mention of it somewhat made up for the intense anxiety this trip would cause me. Apart from Disneyland, I never liked going to amusement parks even as a kid. I didn't like the crowds, the inevitably hot weather and possibility of being stranded on a broken ride at an incredibly high elevation. I preferred a trip to the country with my favorite great-aunt.

Aunt Beebie made this list for a reason though. While I see obviously, she had some big-ticket (literally) items, like Venice, the Northern Lights, etc. I also see Aunt Beebie had some scary things as well. She pushed herself out of her comfort zone. I needed to do the same.

"Ok let's do it. I need to map it out to see how long it'll take, but yes, let's go to the amusement park you see on TV every day."

"Yaaaaayyyyyy!" Logan and Livia cried in absolute joy.

Yes. Yaaaaaayyyyyy. I thought to myself.

Once I figured out the route on my Maps app, we packed our bags, the dog, snacks and plenty of entertainment to get us through the long five-hour drive. When I was younger a five-hour road trip was nothing. Load up on some caffeine and it was over quick. Now that I have three kids (let's face it, George is one of the kids) who all need to potty at different times, are hungry at different times, have meltdowns at different times (yes George has meltdowns too) a five-hour trip feels more like an eight-hour trip.

It was 9:00 in the morning and we arrived at the amusement park at 5:00pm. Just in time for it to close in four hours. Since I was now rich, I didn't have to stay in the economy hotel down the street. I splurged and got us the Family Suite on site at the park.

I had to admit, the splurge was so worth it. Unlimited, complimentary entertainment on the television. Large beds for everyone. Kid friendly snacks and beverages filled the mini bar that was also inclusive with our upgraded suite. Anything we could have possibly needed was at our fingertips. I secretly wished the kids would be so enamored with the room they wouldn't want to leave.

"Mommy, I love this room! Let's go on the rollercoasters now!" Livia shouted from the other side of the room while bouncing effortlessly on her bed.

"Yeah!!!! Let's go!!!!!" Logan also shouted as he jumped from bed to bed. The people below were going to love us.

We stepped out of the hotel into the park in an instant. It was so convenient. And rainy. It was also quite rainy.

"Logan, you need to zip up your raincoat. You're going to get wet otherwise, my love."

"I don't want to."

"Mommy!! I can't get my zipper zipped up! Mommy!! Mommeeeeeee!!!" Livia was in full force panic now.

"Livia! You just need to zip it!" Logan shouted.

"I ammmmmmmm!"

"Obviously you aren't."

"Logan that isn't helping. Zip up your own

jacket."

"I don't want to."

At this point, the rain had decided to come down in full force as though it fed off our frenzied situation.

"Ma'am," a young park employee said to me. "I'm sorry to disturb you. We are asking our guests to take cover. The sirens have started and we're in a tornado threat." The young park worker ushered us out of the open to the hotel banquet room that also served as a tornado shelter. Oh, Aunt Beebie, this is why I don't go on adventures!!!

"Mommy will we go to Oz? I'm scared. I don't want the tornado." Livia had just started to show interest in the Wizard of Oz which at the time, delighted me. Now, not so much.

"No baby. This is just a precaution. There isn't a tornado right now. Just a bad storm."

I was thinking about George, alone in our room. She doesn't like bad weather. I was sure there would be smelly presents left for us upon our return.

An older man in a suit came out from the shadows of safety with a cordless microphone and handful of papers.

"Okay everyone, it looks like we're in the clear. The park is closed though, for the rest of the night so we can assess any damage. We would like to provide a voucher to any of our five restaurants and bars."

I selfishly was happy the park was closed for

the night. After our tornado fright, I needed some French Fries and a Prosecco.

Naturally, the closest spot to eat was a cute Irish Pub which automatically made me think of Deacon. Cute, hot, sensitive Deacon from somewhere outside of Dublin. If I am being totally honest, I've been thinking about him since the morning he dropped me off at my house.

I can't imagine what he would think of my life. He's a young bachelor. I'm a 40-year-old mother of two awesome albeit high maintenance kids. Aren't they all? Oh, who am I kidding? I'm probably just as high maintenance as Logan, Livia and sometimes George.

We walked back to our room where I prepped the kids for what we may come back to.

"Kids, George was alone in our room when all the sirens and weather were in full force. There's a good chance she'll be a bit nervous around us. She may have also pooped or peed somewhere in the room. Let's be careful when we walk in."

"Ew." Logan said, drawing the hoodie part of his sweatshirt onto his head.

I took the magnetic key card from my purse, inhaled what might be my last breath of "fresh" hotel air and walked into the room with the kids. There, on top of my pillow, was a peaceful George, happily sleeping. It was as though she had no idea, we had a possible tornado on the horizon. She didn't leave any smelly presents. In fact, I think George was completely oblivious to it all. Perhaps all amusement parks were truly magical places.

The following day was clear and beautiful. My wild and carefree children had a fabulous time eating amusement park food and going on fast and only somewhat high rides. I had a wonderful time as well. Their father had been gone for a little over two years now. It was hard for them. I tried desperately to be everything they needed and yet seemed to fall short a lot of the time. This trip I saw my children smile freely.

Once everyone had enough fun at the amusement park, we packed our bags back into the car and headed back home. They had plans to meet up with their grandparents, so we didn't have time to stay another night. It was a five-hour drive home to pick up a few things, plus an additional hour or so to meet up with their grandparents.

"Kids, are you excited to go see Grandma and Grandpa? I'm sure they're excited for you to visit." I asked, trying to engage in some sort of conversation, being the only human in the front seat. George is a nice companion, but she just doesn't talk much, being a dog and all.

"I can't wait to play in the treehouse Grandpa made for the backyard. I'm bringing my Nerf guns and we can have battles from there." Logan said, as he ate his turkey sandwich, we purchased from the hotel café earlier.

"I want to bring a Nerf gun! Mommy, do I have Nerf gun?" Asked Livia, who had chosen not to eat a turkey sandwich, or a premade salad or a cheese sandwich, but finally agreed to fresh strawberries.

"Liv, I have a bunch of Nerf guns. You can use one of mine."

"Logan, that's nice. You're a good brother." Logan blushed at my compliment and went back to watching his movie.

"Grandma said she went to the craft store and found a bunch of fun things you guys could do while you're there." I mentioned as we pulled off the highway and entered our city. In addition to being a music teacher, the kids' grandmother also has a very accomplished Pinterest account to showcase her arts and crafts.

"Mommy, I'm going to make you something. Maybe a pretty card, or a turkey or maybe a book. Grandma will help me. She's good at crafts and stuff."

"Those all sound wonderful, Livia. Thank you. I'm sure your grandma has lots of fun ideas as well. She'll help you with whatever you decide to do."

Since Steve's death, I didn't have a strong relationship with his parents. There was not falling out, but we lived different lives and no longer shared a connection with their son anymore. We easily determined early on, Logan and Livia would have plenty of quality time with them. I really didn't want to be without my children for Thanksgiving, but they hadn't seen their grandparents for a few months. Once the school year hits, we're all so busy. My father-in-law is a school Principal and my mother-in-law is busy with her music teaching. We agreed they could go visit during the break for a few nights. We have a nice halfway point where we meet, have lunch and then I leave the kids to finish the trip with their grandparents.

That left me alone for Thanksgiving.

One benefit to being alone for the night is the opportunity to order Thai food delivery without being judged by two children who hate everything that doesn't come with fries.

When I got back home, I sent Cassie a text to let her know I was home and wanted to have a quiet Thanksgiving Day alone tomorrow. Cassie proceeded to return my text with a frantic phone call.

"What do you mean you're staying home alone for Thanksgiving? That's ridiculous!" Cassie was having no part of my nonsense.

"Cassie, it's fine. I'll get up, have some coffee and watch the parade and dog show in peace and quiet. I'm actually looking forward to it."

"Tilda, you need to come over to my house. Deacon will be there." Oh god she said it. She said his name. I hoped she didn't hear my sharp inhale at the sound.

"Cassie, it's very rare I get a moment to myself. It's not a big deal."

"Okay. I can't force you. Please promise me though that any moment you feel lonely, any moment at all, you'll come over. It doesn't matter if it's in the middle of dinner. Do you promise?"

"Yes, Cassie. I promise."

"Ok fine. I'll text you tomorrow to check in and

find out if the parade was everything you thought it would be and more."

"I would expect nothing less from you."

"All right. So, we're clear, Deacon will be disappointed. Okay bye."

When driving home from the road trip with the kids, I thought about Deacon and resolved going on a date with him was a terrible idea. I had absolutely no business entertaining any sort of dealings with that delightful man. Was he a man? Is 28 old enough to be a man? God, he smelled so good, even at 7:00 am after working in a bar the night before.

I woke up on Thanksgiving morning bright and refreshed. George decided not to wake me up in the middle of the night, so my sleep was completely undisturbed. A rare happening, I assure you.

I drank my coffee in peace while watching the Macy's parade. I took a nice long bubble bath. Ate a sandwich. Drank some more coffee. Watched the dog show only to be disappointed in their winner, yet again. Dusted a bit. Then took a nap.

It was a very eventful day.

I woke up from my nap around 5:00 pm to the doorbell ringing. I remembered I'd planned on getting that camera doorbell and wished for it now. Maybe it was Cassie coming to check on me.

I lazily got up to open the door only to be surprised. It wasn't Cassie.

"Deacon! I wasn't expecting you."

"I come bearing gifts from your dear friend. She

insisted I bring you over some leftovers from dinner. Shall I come in?" he asked, hands full of Cassie's care package. Dammit Cassie. He was quite the care package, indeed.

I subtly checked my post nap breath and attempted to smooth my hair. Shit, is that rough patch on my face from drool?? I couldn't seem to get a break when it came to this guy. Couldn't he ever see me when I wasn't a mess?

"Cass wasn't sure if you preferred turkey or ham, so she sent over both. Do you want me to make a plate for you?" He was unloading the dishes from the bag as though it was perfectly natural for him to be here.

I stood and stared, with tears welling up, starting to stream down my face.

"Tilda? Tilda what's wrong? Did I do something wrong? Do you not like either? Oh shit. Are you vegetarian? Cassie should..."

"No, I'm a carnivore!" I said through my blubbers. "It's just. It's just. I haven't had a man in my kitchen since my husband died. Except the plumber. He doesn't count, though. He's 70."

Deacon's face softened. He gently put down the food in his hand and walked over to me. His strong arms enveloped my body and he gave me a warm embrace. We stood in the middle of my kitchen while his warm breath tickled my neck. He just held me.

"Tilda, I'm sorry." Deacon whispered softly in my ear.

"It's okay Deacon. It isn't your fault."

"Can I get you a drink? I think Cassie put some wine in here for you."

"Sure, thank you. I promise I won't get drunk and attack you this time."

"Well that's disappointing." He winked as he poured my glass of Chardonnay. Bless her. Cassie not only sent me food with a hot man, she also sent my preferred wine.

I could feel my face burning as Deacon poured my wine. My heart pounded and I could barely breathe. I didn't understand how a stranger could have such an effect on me. He didn't feel like a stranger though. He felt like someone I'd known forever.

"Where are your kids? Don't you have a couple?" Deacon looked around as though he remembered we had children nearby.

"I let them stay with their grandparents for a few days. They live a couple of hours away, so the kids don't get to see them as often as they'd like."

"Hmm. So, you get to have some time to yourself then? Am I intruding?" he asked as he poured another glass of wine for himself.

"No, you aren't. Truth be told, I've been a bit bored and lonely today. Don't tell Cassie. It's funny, when there's nothing but chaos all I want is a break, and when I get it, I find the quiet is almost unbearable. Ugh, here I go again."

Good grief! He must think I'm such a downer! Stop talking, Tilda!

"Do you miss him a lot? Your husband?"

"I miss the idea of him."

"What do you mean?"

"My husband wasn't the person I thought he was. I thought he was a loyal husband and family man who worked hard to take care of us. Alas, I was mistaken. He was in a car accident nearly three years ago. Killed on impact. He wasn't the only one in the car. His work trip was in fact, a getaway in Napa with his mistress. His death was how I found about the affair."

"Holy shit, Tilda. That's bloody awful. What did you tell your kids?" He seemed genuinely dumbfounded. That reaction is rather typical.

"My kids know nothing about the affair. I have no intention of them knowing either."

Deacon nodded his head in agreement and gently changed the subject as he topped off my glass of wine.

"So, tell me more about this bucket list."

"Well, I have several things left to check off, that's for sure. My Aunt Beebie didn't get to complete it, so she left it for me to do the rest. She also wants me to finish it in a year."

"I think you've done quite well so far. Anymore kissing strange men on there?"

I laughed at his question and handed him a copy of the list that I left on the end table. I knew he'd gotten to the 'pose nude' when he laughed.

"Have you ever posed nude before?"

"Um no. What do you think? That I was a Playboy model in my past life? I don't like being naked ever. EVER. I have no idea how I'll get through that one."

"What about dancing. Do you know how to dance already?"

"Nope. Unless you count the booty shaking of the 90s."

"Hm. I could be wrong, but I think your aunt may have meant something more formal. I could teach you a bit if you like. As it happens, my mother made me take dance lessons as a lad. She thought it would refine me a bit."

"Did it? Refine you?" I couldn't help but be amused at the idea of a young, scrappy Deacon taking an elegant dance class.

"What do you think?"

"I'd say you're more refined than a lot of guys I've met."

Deacon stood up and gallantly approached me, "Well thank you, Tilda. Now, how about that dance?"

"What dance?" I asked, confused.

"Don't you want to learn how to dance? I think we have enough space here for a waltz." Deacon scanned the room a bit, moving an ottoman further over to the side of the room.

"A waltz?!"

Deacon pulled me closer and said, "Follow my lead. You'll be fine. Do you have Alexa?"

"Yes."

"Alexa, play 'The Way You Look Tonight.' He

smiled and gave me his signature wink. God that wink.

Alexa responded, "Playing the Way You Look Tonight by Tony Bennett."

"Okay Tilda. 1-2-3. 1-2-3. Yep, that's it."

We danced in my living room to Tony Bennett until the song ended. He looked at me with his beautiful eyes and touched the side of my face. Softly. I thought I would collapse at that very moment. I didn't collapse though. Deacon held me and kissed me in a way that I could never drink enough wine to forget. Even in my oldest of age I don't think I'll ever lose this memory.

"Oh my." It was all I could say.

"Tilda."

"Yes," I said passionately in his embrace.

"Tilda, you're on my foot."

I stepped back, embarrassed. "Oh! Sorry! I guess I was caught up in it all. This is the first time I've kissed a man since, well, in a very long time."

"No need to apologize." He said with a smile. "I should probably get going though. If I stay any longer... well... I should probably get going." Deacon let out a deep breath and stared at me for a moment. I didn't want him to leave. I wanted him to stay and hold me. I wanted him to keep me company in this quiet house of just George and me. I didn't tell him that though. He was probably right anyway. If he stayed, we would likely have sex, which I was not remotely ready for.

We exchanged numbers and he kissed me goodbye. I went to bed shortly after and had wonderful dreams of a handsome Irishman.

Chapter 6

Now that Thanksgiving had passed, it was officially the Christmas season. The kids were busy writing, editing, rewriting and completely changing their lists for Santa. Every time a new commercial aired, or another toy catalogue arrived in the mail, new lists were compiled.

Besides my children's Christmas list, the only other list I could focus on was my bucket list. I was training for a long-distance run; okay it was the *New Year, New You* 5K but for me that is plenty long distance. Aunt Beebie didn't specify what type and since I was taking over the bucket list, I decided she would find 3.107 miles perfectly acceptable. Despite my legs, lungs and bladder feeling otherwise.

The surprising thing out of all of this was my trainer. It was none other than the wicked Tabitha Wells. Since making amends, we have texted back and forth, and she has talked to me about her job as a personal trainer. This explained her pink sports drinks and athleisure wear every day. The bouncy ponytail I think was just because of good genes.

We had spoken more about Aunt Beebie's bucket list and Tabitha kindly offered to help me train for my 5K. We had been meeting at the park by our kids' school to train. After this morning however, I decided she may still be wicked.

"Tilda, you can't expect to run three miles if

you haven't worked your muscles in, how many years is it? Six?"

"I still don't understand why climbing my stairs at home doesn't count for anything. Do you know how many times a day I have to go up and down those blessed things?!" For a while, I tried out one of the fitness watches to see exactly how sedentary I was. I found myself shocked to discover I wasn't sedentary at all! Tending to my children's never-ending needs kept my steps well over 15,000. That's above the national average according to Google.

"Stairs don't count. Now drop and give me 20 burpees." She said in between shouts of "Today Tilda! The 5K is in a few weeks!" and "Don't you want to have a rockin' bod when you get that Irish boy in bed? Work it!"

"I'm dead. I'm officially dead and I'm going to haunt you forever, Tabitha Wells."

"Yes. You also weigh five pounds less and can run a mile. I'm doing my job, I think."

I whimpered to my car. She was right. I had lost a few pounds and was slightly less embarrassed of my body. Although Deacon and I had been casually seeing one another for a couple of weeks, we still had not made it to *that* point. Innocent making out only. I'm not in college anymore. I am a respectable grown up. Well, attempting to be anyway.

In addition to my torturous exercise with Tabitha, I was also taking a beginner ballroom dance class at the community center. It was mostly senior citizens and a few newly engaged couples, but there was one other person sans dancing partner. My new friend, Kyle.

Kyle was a twenty-something guy who was very sweet, and possibly a worse dancer than me. He told me in our first class, last week, that he was taking the dance class solo to impress his girlfriend, who was a wonderful dancer. Eventually, Kyle wanted to show off his dance moves during a romantic proposal to his love, Sarah. He was so nervous and sweaty tonight, if he proposed to Sarah right now, he might possibly collapse from sweat dehydration.

"Now, gentlemen keep your head up, eyes forward. Yes, that's it. You are the leaders in this romantic interlude." Our dance instructor, Ms. Bolivar proclaimed as she went around the room, adjusting hands and heads. When she came to us, I was quite certain I saw an eye roll.

"Kyle, darling, if you breathe, I think you will find it much easier to do your counts." She patted Kyle on the back as she moved on to the other more competent dancers.

Ms. Bolivar was a petite lady who was not afraid to be direct yet had a kind way of being so. She looked to be around 60, but her black hair wasn't having any of that. It sat tightly on her head in a full and elegant bun. The silk chiffon skirt of her beautiful tea length dress swayed as she glided across the room. I imagined in her youth Ms. Bolivar could have been a star in her own right. You can tell that type of person, I think. They have a way of holding their head high, with confidence and determination. I wished I could be more like Ms. Bolivar.

"Kyle, are you okay? You seem extra nervous." To be clear, Kyle was never not nervous. I didn't need to point that out to the kid though.

"I'm meeting my hopefully future father-in-law tonight after class for a beer at the pub down the street. I'm going to ask him for permission to propose to Sarah. My girlfriend. My girlfriend, Sarah." Kyle rambled on, getting more nervous the more he spoke.

"Kyle, that's wonderful!" I exclaimed. "What an honorable thing to do."

"He's terrifying. Sarah worships him and tells me he's a big teddy bear, but I haven't seen that side of him. He mostly just grunts at me, you know, like The Mountain in Game of Thrones?"

"Well if he's that protective of his daughter, I can't imagine he'd continue to approve of your dating if there wasn't some sort of approval. Not to mention Kyle, you're both adults. How old are you?"

"We're both 29."

"You're 29?" I was shocked to think Kyle was even older than Deacon. His baby face and less confident demeanor led me to assume he wasn't more than 23. Deacon, on the other hand at least looked 28, possibly older. I wished anyway.

"Yes. We've been together since our senior year

of high school."

"Hold up. You've been in a relationship with this girl for like, 11 years, and all you've gotten are grunts from her father?"

Kyle gulped and began to breathe harder before he almost passed out. "Yes. Well, once I got a 'uh-huh' grunt when I wished him a happy birthday."

I could see he was in a terrible state and guided him over to the bench for a rest and hydration.

"Here, have a sip of water. You can't meet him looking like this. What time are you supposed to be there?"

"We're meeting at 7:00," he said in a higher pitch.

I looked at the clock which read 6:35. Not much time to fix the hot mess that stood before me, but it was worth a shot.

"Ok, we need to hurry. Come on." I let Ms. Bolivar know we had an emergency that required us to leave. She waved us off and continued her focus on counting steps. I also sent a text to Cassie, letting her know the situation. She texted me back immediately, saying the kids were perfectly fine and having a great time...and to keep her posted.

We exited the community center building quickly. Kyle followed me to my car, and we sped away. Unfortunately, the speed limit downtown was only 25 miles per hour, so we didn't speed off as fast as I'd have preferred.

"Where are we going?" Kyle asked, nervously.

"Can you text The Mountain and ask him to

meet you at 7:30?" I asked, maneuvering through pedestrians and double-parked delivery trucks.

"Change the plans?! I don't know!" He fiddled with his phone and tensely texted his future father-in-law to push his meeting back 30 minutes.

"Kyle, just do it. We need to clean you up first. You can't meet your future father-in-law looking like this. God, what were you thinking? You look like you just swam the English Channel with all that sweat."

"Okay he responded. Yes. Okay so what now?" Kyle's breathing seemed to slow down a bit and his shaking subdued.

"I'm taking you to my house. We're almost there. I have a bunch of nice clothes that were my late husband's I think they will work for you."

"He won't mind?"

"Kyle, he's dead. I should have probably donated them a long time ago. He won't mind."

We pulled into my driveway, where I ushered him into the downstairs bathroom, to take a quick shower to wash the desperation off his body.

I scoured the spare bedroom closet where I kept my husband's clothes. I was never ready to part with them. If this were a Lifetime movie, I would have torched them on his ridiculously large backyard grill. I should have, given everything he did to me. Despite the deceit and betrayal, I still had a difficult time parting with some of his things.

I found a nice tweed blazer and a Hugo Boss

collared shirt that would complement Kyle's dark features and hair. Pants were a no-go because Kyle was taller than my husband. A quick steam from his shower and a spritz of fabric spray solved that problem.

"Kyle, if you asked for my daughter's hand in marriage I would say yes. Well, not *my* daughter's hand, because she's six but, you know what I mean."

"Thank you, Tilda. I don't know that he'll be any more impressed with me, but he won't be less." Kyle gave me a hug and then looked at his watch. "I have to go! I can't be late!!"

We hopped in the car so I could drop him off at the pub.

Realizing I had no idea where I was racing off to, I said, "I forgot to ask, what's the name of the pub?"

"Brodies's. It's right down the street from the community center. I parked my car there and walked to class."

"Hmmmm. I have a friend working there right now. Maybe I could stay for a bit. You know, for moral support. Also, as a witness if he slams a sledgehammer down on the table." My attempt at humor suddenly created a bead of sweat down Kyle's face. "Never mind! Drink some water. Here's a tissue. It'll be fine." Shit, how scary was this guy?

I parked my car and we walked into Brodie's. It was a Wednesday night, yet busy because it was a Well-Night with $3 whisky shots and $2 draft beers. I saw a table of ladies who seemed to be taking advantage of the joyous alcohol sale. Hopefully the plates of fries and calamari would soak up the copious amounts of alcohol was in their system, based on the empty shot glasses on their table. I felt a pang of jealousy as I watched them ogle Deacon as he poured drinks.

'Sweaty Kyle' started to rear his clammy head and said, "He's over there. Oh god, I can't do this Tilda."

"Yes, you can. Just remember the reason. You love Sarah." The idea of his love calmed his face and leveled his breathing and, hopefully, his perspiration. Man, that kid could sweat. Kyle walked away to the table that seated a giant of a man and greeted him with confidence and poise.

I spotted Deacon at the bar and took a seat.

"Hey! What are you doing here? On a school night no less? Miss me that much?" He asked as he wiped the counter down and handed me a bowl of sesame pub mix.

"If you must know, I'm here helping a friend. See that big guy over there? His future son-in-law is about to ask permission to marry his daughter." I told him the story, picking out the extra crunchy bits in my savory snack.

"People still do that, ask for permission?" Deacon asked perplexed.

"Yes, people still do that! It's polite and romantic, I think." My husband didn't do that. My father died when I was young, and my mother was in a nursing home.

"Ah good to know. I'll bring him over a drink. You think he's a Guinness man like his future father-in-law?" Deacon asked as he poured the heavy dark beverage from a tap.

"Well he is now-- if he's smart. Send over two." I slid a $5 bill over to Deacon and said, "They're on me."

Deacon placed the two drinks on the table as the men continued their conversation. We tried to watch inconspicuously, desperate to find out what the answer would be. I found Deacon's interest endearing. He was as fascinated by the whole scene as me, especially the dynamic between Kyle and The Mountain man.

Mountain was an accurate description of the man. He looked to be close to seven feet tall and possibly the same in width. He didn't look incredibly fat, just solid. Any evidence of a double chin was masked by a thick, dark beard. I could understand the fear Kyle was bottling up for so long

The Mountain man stood up with his Guinness and let out his signature grunt. "Can I have your attention? This man has just asked my permission to wed my only daughter. What do you think, everyone? Should I say yes?"

Kyle's face was beet red and his sweat was coming back. I mimed a breathing exercise we practiced in the car. He seemed to regain a less crimson pallor once the oxygen travelled back to his head.

The audience cheered. The Mountain man raised his glass and yelled, "To Sarah and Kyle and

Bob, that's me!" Phew. I shuddered to think what would've happened had the opposite response transpired. Once I learned his name was Bob, his intimidation factor kind of went down a bit. Not that there is anything wrong with the name, it's just The Mountain has a far more intense reaction.

Deacon smiled and said, "Well it looks like your friend has the luck of the Guinness."

"Thank the heavens. He's been my dancing partner at class. Now that he got the necessary approval, maybe he won't step on my toes as much." If only, I thought, I could get the luck of the Guinness and stop stepping on Kyle's toes…

Chapter 7

Deacon took a break to walk me to my car. The temperature had seemed do go down 20 degrees since I'd been inside. I didn't mind though. It gave me an excuse to walk down the street with Deacon close by my side.

I wished I didn't feel the way I felt. Despite his maturity and kindness, I still worried he was too young. Was I falling for a guy that just wanted to have fun? He made it so difficult, being absolutely amazing and all.

"That was a lovely thing you did tonight, Tilda, helping that fella." Deacon said giving my hand a soft squeeze.

"Oh, I don't know. I think it would've turned out the same way regardless. That future father-in-law enjoys terrifying poor Kyle. He couldn't possibly have said no though. His daughter has dated the kid for a decade!"

"I wonder why it took him this long to propose. On second thought, maybe I do."

I laughed at the thought of poor Kyle and his predicament, "Did you see the state he was in? He could probably do himself a favor and take up meditation. He's a sweet guy, but he's a wreck."

Deacon laughed quietly and said, "You may be right."

"Well, I think I should probably get back. My kids have been with Cassie for a lot longer than I expected and it's a school night. Oh jeez, I forgot to do Livia's reading assignment with her before I left for class. She's not doing well with her reading lately. Shit!"

"Tilda one night isn't going to send your daughter back to kindergarten."

I was sure he was right. My mom guilt kicked into full force. I wanted to be there for my kids at all times, whenever they needed me. Unrealistic... yes. On my list of to-do's...every waking moment.

Deacon gave me one of his sweet smiles and a long kiss. I felt like he wanted to say more to me, but he had to get back to work. He'd left his co-worker, Deshawn alone. Normally that would've been fine. However, Kyle's future father-in-law Bob, AKA The Mountain, had purchased a round of drinks for the entire bar. Thankfully for me, Deshawn was also a gentleman and didn't want me to walk to my car alone in the dark of night.

I pulled up to Cassie's house at about 8:30. She recently had a professional landscaper do her front yard, so I was most definitely not in the dark. Beautiful spotlights highlighted her perfect lawn and flowerbeds. I must admit, I was rather envious. I have no idea how to keep a lawn looking like it's May in January. Now that I had a few million dollars in the bank, maybe I would hire Cassie's yard man.

I was still in denial and shock that I had millions of dollars in the bank.

I rang Cassie's fancy doorbell and she opened

the door immediately. I imagined her with frizzy auburn hair, covered with toy slime, but alas, she looked perfectly normal. Nothing seems to ever faze my dear friend.

"How'd it go? Did everything turn out ok?" Cassie walked me into the back room, where all four kids were hanging out with blankets, hot chocolates, watching a gripping episode of The Amazing World of Gumball.

"The father said yes and bought drinks for everybody. It was nice. I got to see Deacon as well, so it was a bonus!" I still felt like I blushed whenever I mentioned his name out loud.

"Oh, that boy has fallen head over heels for you, Tilda. He blushes more than you when I mention you. I wish he wasn't going back home so soon."

"What do you mean back home? Your home in the back yard or his *somewhere outside of Dublin* home?" I suddenly felt like I was going to vomit.

"Uh, oh. Uh." Cassie stuttered. She obviously let something out of the bag. "I'm sorry, Tilda. Deacon just found out. I thought he'd told you right away. I'm sorry."

"Cassie! What is happening? Why does he have to go back to Ireland??" I knew it. I knew just when I let my guard down something like this would happen.

"He got a call and was kind of upset. He didn't go into detail with me, so I don't know. Maybe his Visa?

"When does he go back home?"

"I think in a few weeks. I'm not sure. I'm sorry, Tilda. He can explain it better than I can."

I fought to hold back any emotion that would show just how devastated I was. Nothing serious had been discussed between us and I knew in my gut we were just having a fling. Yet, here I was on the verge of tears imagining not seeing Deacon again.

"No, Cassie. I'm sorry. I shouldn't be giving you the third degree. It's Deacon who needs to explain it all." I took a few breaths in and out and quickly changed my focus back to my kids.

"Okay, guys, it's time to go," I said, grabbing their coats.

"Mom it's not over yet! I don't want to go home!" Logan shouted from Cassie's sofa. How did she keep it so clean? Her sheer brazenness of giving kids hot chocolate on a cream-colored sofa astounded me. That's why we were friends. She always astounds me. In a good way, of course.

"Logan, I'm sure you can find it another day to finish watching it. Besides, it probably goes something like, Gumball and Darwin do something stupid; they upset some of their strange friends; then, by the skin of their teeth, Gumball and Darwin fix the stupid action and everything is back to normal. Now let's go. You guys have school tomorrow."

Livia chimed in and said, "Mama that's not what happened! Gumball's dad did something stupid. And it was funny." Ah yes, the stupid dad. Truth is, I've watched the show with them, and it is mesmerizing. I usually have absolutely no idea what's happening, but I can't stop watching.

I said goodbye to my dear friend and got the kids in the car. Although we only live a few streets away, Livia was already asleep by the time I pulled into the garage. Logan was grumpy and refused to brush his teeth, which I didn't fight. One night of a mouth bacteria party was not going to send him to dentures and I didn't have the energy to fight about it.

Once the kids were in bed and George got some much-needed attention, I took a shower and got in bed myself. I couldn't sleep though. Mostly because Deacon kept texting me. I did not want to talk about it.

RU up?

Sorry to hear ur leaving. Talk about later? Thx.

I'm sorry. I didn't have a chance to tell u.

Deacon it's fine. Goodnight.

Talk in morning?

Sure. Maybe. I might be running. 5K race to do. Goodnight.

Goodnight.

Once I finally fell asleep, I did not sleep well. Even worse, all of my Deacon drama caused me to forget to set my alarm. The kids woke me up. Unfortunately, it was ten minutes before the tardy bell music starts at their school. I was supposed to meet Tabitha for a run at 8:00 am. Thankfully I showered last night, so I threw on some running clothes, prepared peanut butter sandwiches for the kids to eat in the car, made sure they brushed their teeth before we left since neither did the night before and successfully drove them to school with their to-go breakfast. This also meant walking them in since they were 20 minutes late. Thankfully I was dressed in actual daytime clothes and not pajamas.

Twenty minutes late for the kids meant I was five minutes late for Tabitha. She was at the adjacent park waiting for me. She had on pink fuzzy earmuffs that fit perfectly around her perfect ponytail. I don't know why I'm so jealous of her stupid perfect hair but I am. My dark wavy hair isn't terrible, I just can't get perky ponytails like Tabitha's.

"Okay Tilda, we're doing the entire three miles today. Your run is in a few weeks and you haven't done a total 5K yet."

I resolved that my inner devastation would be my secret power today, and it was. It kept me motivated. I told myself that I didn't have time to waste on a silly romance. I had a job to do. I had a 5K to complete for Aunt Beebie. I had a trip to finish booking for the Alaska Northern Lights in March. There was Venice to plan, assuming it wasn't still under water. Thanks a lot, climate change.

We started out with our stretches and then began a slow jog down the street and through the neighborhood.

Tabitha was in much better shape than I was, but my determination kept my legs going. It was cold outside, and my face stung a bit in the frigid air. However, it was important for me to know I could actually do a 5K run and not fall down half-way through. I imagined Aunt Beebie would have had the same determination. Sometimes, when I was little, we would do fun jazzercise routines at her house. I don't recall ever seeing her run though. Perhaps that's what led her to adding a long-distance race to her bucket list. Perhaps she wanted to show herself she could do things she'd never thought of doing.

"We're almost there, Tilda. Let's finish strong. Come on you can do it!"

My lungs were tight from the cold and being worked. My legs were jelly and I just wanted to lay down, but I kept going.

"Tilda, that was incredible. You finished and kept up with me the whole time!" Tabitha said between freezing cold breaths.

"I didn't think I could do it, Tabitha. Thank you for your help. It really means a lot to me. You're not as much of a bitch as I thought."

We laughed and decided to get breakfast at the new café around the corner.

The restaurant was cute, with 50s era décor. Our server led us to our table and took our order. I was starving from just finishing my "long distance run" so naturally, I ordered something hearty.

"Okay, Tilda, I'm dying to hear. What's going on

with your boy toy?" Tabitha asked as she sipped her super healthy green tea. While I drank coffee with half and half.

"Nothing. Apparently, he's going back to Ireland. Cassie told me last night."

Her eyes widened, "He's leaving, and he didn't tell you?!" Her eyes were wide and interested as she dipped her spoon into the bowl of steel cut oatmeal.

"No. I'm not sure when this all transpired, but no. He didn't. Now he's been blasting me with text messages wanting to talk. I keep trying to ignore it, but he won't let me. I finally told him to leave me alone. I was trying to have breakfast with you." I dove into my Eggs Benedict with furious resolve, sopping up every ounce of hollandaise sauce with each bite.

"Why don't you at least let him explain? What's it going to hurt?"

I wanted to scream, ME THAT'S WHAT! I was still guarded though.

"I know I need to talk to him. I will. I just have a lot going on. This list isn't going away and I owe it myself and my Aunt Beebie to focus on it. Did I tell you I found an incredible deal on a luxury Alaskan Northern Lights adventure for the kids and I?"

"Ooh no! I've always wanted to see the Northern Lights!"

"Well, we're going in March. We'll fly into Anchorage. Then in the early hours of the morning or late hours of the night, there's a shuttle that takes

us about 20 miles away where we
may or may not get to see the lights."

"What do you mean, 'may or may not'? You might take the whole trip and not even get to see them?!"

I shrugged, as I drank my coffee and said, "I guess Mother Nature can be persnickety." I thought it was crazy as well, but I had to at least try.

"Ahem." A deep, male voice cleared in my background. Tabitha almost choked on her egg white & kale omelet.

"What are you doing here? I told you I was busy."

Deacon brushed his hands through his hair and said quietly but firmly, "Tilda, we need to talk."

"Well I'm just so busy right now. I'm having breakfast with Tabitha. I've been training and all. We're focusing on our high protein and healthy carb meal, right Tabitha?"

Tabitha's eyes widened and added, "Yes! Tilda finished her 5K practice this morning! She had some major determination this morning. Err, I forgot. I have a training session I'm late for. Excuse me. Text me later, Tilda. Bye... uh, bye." Tabitha threw down a $20 for her breakfast and practically ran out of the restaurant.

Deacon slid into Tabitha's side of the booth and said, "Tilda, I'm sorry. I wanted to tell you last night. I just didn't know how. Then I got home, and Cassie told me she said something...it's just a mess Tilda. I'm devastated."

His eyes expressed everything they needed to.

"I'm devastated, too. Deacon, I haven't been completely honest with you about my feelings. I know we've been playing this like it's casual and fun. But the thing is, I'm not a casual and fun kind of girl."

"Go on."

"I like stability. I like monogamy. I like knowing I have someone to come home to each day. I didn't want to scare you off. I know you're so much younger than me and you're in a totally different place. But I'm falling for you, Deacon. And now, you have to leave me." I couldn't hide my pain anymore. I started to tear up and as I turned my face up to his, I saw the same emotion.

I assumed our feelings weren't mutual. That he was a playboy just out to have fun. It didn't occur to me that my young, carefree Deacon felt exactly the same way.

He moved over to my bench and held my face, firmly, while kissing me with passion and love.

"Tilda, I'm falling for you. Hard. And if I have to go back home to Ireland to make sure I never have to leave you again, that's what I'll do. If you'll wait for me."

"Yes. I'll wait for you. If you promise to come back to me. Do you promise Deacon Kelly? If I give my heart to you, do you promise to come back to me?"

"Yes." We made out a bit more in the restaurant before realizing people were trying to eat their pancakes. *Gross*, I thought to myself.

I wanted to completely ignore that voice in my head telling me to wrap this up and go to the grocery store for more Cosmic Brownies like a good mother should.

"Shall we take this back to my house?"

"Yes, I could do with a nap. Didn't sleep much last night."

"That wasn't really what I had in mind, although I do love a good nap..."

I paid the breakfast bill while Deacon sped off in his car, to meet me at my house for a nap.

I sat up in my bed which besides me, has only occupied my kids and George for the last three years. It was a strangely comfortable feeling to have a man next me. His warm body at ease from our previous interlude. I always imagined any future love making would be awkward given how long it had been. I can tell you it wasn't. It was ahhhhhmazing.

Deacon rolled over to his side and asked, "So Tilda, what's next on your bucket list? Does it include any trips to Ireland to kiss a fella?"

"Hmmm, no Ireland. Although there is a trip to Venice. Any interest in meeting me there? Perhaps a rendezvous at the quite romantic London Heathrow Airport?"

He smiled and replied, "Sounds fantastic. Never been to Italy. I think I could arrange something. I'll go back to the pub I worked at before to save up some money. I've got to figure out a way to get back to The States though. I'm just not sure when I can do that. It's rather complicated."

I realized I never told Deacon about my recent pot of gold. I've been so much in denial that it mostly sits in my bank account. It has covered a few bills for me because I haven't been terribly motivated to take on new work projects since my life has been flipped upside down.

"Actually, I'd like to treat you to this trip. If you don't mind."

"Oh no, Tilda. I couldn't accept that. I can pay my own way. You have a lot more responsibilities than I do at the moment."

"What if I told you my financial responsibilities are in perfect shape?"

He looked at me, perplexed and said, "Go on."

"Well, my Aunt Beebie apparently was quite rich. She didn't spend a lot of money in her later years. I've recently been given a few million dollars. Well, $2.8 million to be precise."

Deacon coughed, "2.8 million dollars? Holy shit, Tilda!"

"I know. That was my reaction as well. I need to get a financial advisor so I can figure out how to invest some of it. I need to start a college savings for Logan and Liv, and that type of thing."

"I still can't ask you to pay my way."

"Well I plan on taking this trip in first class comfort. Will you at least let me pay for your upgrades and accommodations?"

"Only if you let me explore every inch of your

body in the finest Italian linens while we're there." He said as he gently ran his finger along my hip and waist.

"Deal." How could I say no to that? I really needed to exercise harder. If sex made me breathe this much, the 5K might ruin me. Although, they really are apples and oranges.

"My 5K is a couple Saturdays away. Will you still be here?" I asked, trying my hardest to not cry at the thought of him not.

"Let me check the dates when I...leave." Deacon's pause told me he was having a difficult time as well. "My flight leaves the Sunday morning after."

"So, you'll be able to come cheer me on?" I asked from the bathroom as I turned on the shower to warm up the water.

"Absolutely. What time?"

"It starts at 7:00."

"In the morning?"

"Yes, in the morning!"

"My Friday night shift ends at around 2:00 that morning, so that gives me, let me think, a few hours of sleep. Yes, I'll be there for 7:00 to cheer you on. I just may still have a bit of scruff on the face."

"I love your face scruff. And thank you. I appreciate the sleep deprivation for me. There's a good chance you may have to peel me off the ground somewhere,

though. Sadly, a few miles of running might kill

me."

"I know what will help get you in good shape."

"Deacon! I already started the shower."

"We don't have to use the bed. I imagine we can take a care of a few things in your shower."

What was I going to do when he left? Besides the much-needed sex, I was really going to miss him.

Chapter 8

Christmas was finally here and watching the kids tear into their presents was absolute joy for me. Livia still tended to want smaller presents, like dolls; whereas Logan gravitated to higher-priced electronic items. Santa brought George a new dog bed and gourmet treats. All in all, it seemed everyone had a lovely morning.

"Mommy, is Mr. Deacon coming to visit today?" Livia asked, putting a second unicorn headband on top of her head.

"Would you like him to visit? I thought this morning it could just be us. I have cinnamon rolls in the oven for you." I was quite proud of my homemade delights. I woke up extra early to make them.

"But mommy, wouldn't Mr. Deacon like cimmanon rolls?" Livia was still having trouble with some words, and cinnamon was one of them. "Me and Logan think you should text him."

When Logan nodded his head in agreement, I sent a quick text inviting Deacon over for cinnamon rolls and coffee.

"He'll be over in a few minutes, guys. I think he was excited to hear you wanted him to come over."

The kids and I finished cleaning up the Christmas mess of wrapping paper before my handsome Irishman arrived.

The doorbell rang and we greeted Deacon, who

had his hands full of presents.

"Ho, ho, ho!" He said, walking into the house. "I have presents for Logan, Livia, a beautiful lady named Tilda and an equally beautiful lady named, err, George." George's face lit up when she heard the squeaky toy that Deacon threw for her.

"Deacon, you didn't have to do this. How thoughtful." I was utterly shocked that he would bring presents for everyone, including my dog.

The kids opened their Christmas gifts, which included a new Xbox game that Logan has had his eye on and a fabulous Barbie camper for Livia.

The kids ran off to the playroom, shouting, "Thank you!!!!" to Deacon.

Deacon kissed me on the cheek and asked, "Are you going to open your present?"

I carefully removed the wrapping paper to find a long, rectangle box. Inside was a beautiful opal necklace with a long silver chain.

"Oh Deacon, I love it! Thank you."

"You're welcome," he said as he helped me put the opal necklace around my neck.

"Ah, now, where are those cinnamon rolls that were promised to me?"

"Oh! I forgot! Yes, let me help you with that."

We walked to the kitchen, where I prepared a plate with a large cinnamon roll on it and handed him a cup of coffee. "Merry Christmas!" I said, scooting the plate over to him.

Deacon took a bite and said, "Mmmmmm!" with his mouthful of cinnamon rolls. "Merry Christmas, Tilda. These are 'effing delicious."

Deacon finished his cinnamon roll and we moved back to the family room with our coffees. We sat and relaxed on the sofa, watching Christmas movies with the kids for most of the morning. At noon, I told the kids we had to get dressed because Cassie was having us over later. She was very excited to host us, and I was very excited not to have to cook anything besides a baked macaroni and cheese.

It was truly a blessed Christmas.

Now, I just needed to be blessed once more for my upcoming 5Krun. I did not want to let anyone down, especially Aunt Beebie.

Saturday morning arrived, and I was terrified to start my *New Year, New You 5K.* My layers of clothing to run in the frigid 29 degrees helped hide the fact I was wearing lady bladder protection, thanks to pushing two kids out of well...you know. Running isn't really my friend when it comes to that department.

Logan and Livia were bundled up with Cassie and Tabitha and their kids. I was sincerely shocked when Tabitha said she wanted to come. I was still having trouble reconciling that she's not a total bitch.

Deacon hadn't made it yet, but he sent me a text saying he was on his way. He just had to make a quick stop first and then he'd be there soon.

I had to just remember what Cassie and Tabitha told me. Take my time, remember my breathing and maybe start doing more Kegels.

I also had a secret good luck charm, my locket with a sprinkle of Aunt Beebie's ashes. I hoped it would give me an extra boost of confidence and energy, like Aunt Beebie always did, to keep me from finishing last.

When I was little, I would pretend I was an Olympic athlete. Aunt Beebie, as usual, would humor me and praise my skills. In the winter, I would pretend I was an ice skater. In the summer, I would be a gold medal sprinter. My tiny legs would run through her yard as though I were Carl Lewis himself. I obviously wasn't, but my dear aunt would cheer me on just the same. She always cheered me on. No matter how terrible I may have been at something.

While I waited to hear the signal that it was time to run, trying to imagine I was at the house on the hill and the star in Aunt Beebie's eyes.

"On your marks! Get set! Go!"

The loud horn blew, and the race officially began.

I started my run and multiple people, including what appeared to be elementary school children sped past me, heads high. Their little lungs didn't seem to be at all disturbed by the cold temperature or physical activity.

I resolved to not let that bother me. I had to focus on my own pace. Slow. Almost walking.

About a mile in, I began to breathe a bit easier, despite the freezing temperature. At two miles, my legs began to burn, and a solid side cramp started. It was time to walk a bit. No shame in that, I told myself. There were plenty of people who chose to walk. Most of them were about thirty years older than me, but no worries. We're all just people here, trying to finish.

Once my side cramp calmed down, I picked up my pace and was determined to finish this race in less than an hour. As I ran further and further, I could hear the cheers for runners who finished before me.

I was almost there.

"Come on Tilda. Move it." I said out loud to myself. And then I saw him. Deacon, with Cassie, Tabitha, their kids and mine. They were cheering together, excited as though they'd known each other for their whole lives.

Livia was perched on top of Deacon's shoulders with her arms practically strangling his neck. Logan stood next to them, jumping up and down, holding a bouquet of flowers.

I made it. I crossed the finish line and ran to my friends and family. I finished in under an hour. Almost 49 minutes exactly. Not the best time but it was my best time and I felt proud of that. I could feel Aunt Beebie's satisfaction in my heart.

"Mama! You did it!" Logan cheered as he handed me the flowers. Livia got down from Deacon's shoulders and ran to me.

"Mommy!! Yay! Ew. You're all sweaty." Livia is my sensitive yet honest child. She hates strong odors, most textures, dampness included and not being direct.

"Yep. Mommy needs to change her clothes before she gets hypothermia. No, seriously it's freezing out here. Cass, can I borrow your minivan to change?"

Cassie handed me the keys and said, "Got it heated up for ya!"

I changed quickly into some clean, dry clothes and met everyone back outside.

Cassie shouted in excitement, "Everyone is welcome to come back to my place for an after 5K brunch! Since Deacon leaves tomorrow for Dublin, I thought we could enjoy a day together. How about 11:00?"

Tabitha hugged me goodbye and said, "I'd love to, Cassie, but I have a hockey game for Alexi in a couple hours and a workout to squeeze in. You did great, Tilda. I'm proud of you. I'll see you next week at school."

"Thank you, Tabitha, for everything."

"Not a problem, Tilda. It was your hard work and determination that got you to the finish line. Have fun, guys! See you later!"

Cassie eagerly looked at Deacon and me.

"Does 11:00 work?"

"Absolutely!" I said. I was in dire need of a shower and cup of coffee so 11:00 worked perfectly for me.

Livia tugged at Deacon's jacket and asked, "Mr. Deacon, you want to come to our house and watch

SpongeBob?"

"Liv, I bet Mr. Deacon has..."

"Miss Livia, there is nothing I'd rather do. I'm a big SpongeBob fan myself. Who's your favorite? Squidward? Patrick?"

"SpongeBob!" Livia shouted excitedly.

"Well it's settled then. If your mother doesn't mind of course. And guess what? You don't have to call me Mr. Deacon. Deacon is just fine." Deacon, who was still crouched to Livia's level, looked up at me in question.

I looked down at my sweet Livia and my Irish fella and couldn't possibly say no. My heart was still cracking at the idea of him leaving. My inner voice telling me to distance myself, but then again, I couldn't. I wanted to spend every waking moment with Deacon before he left indefinitely.

The kids headed back to our house with Cassie since she drove us to the race and the booster seats were in her car. I drove with Deacon.

"That was really sweet, the way you were with Livia."

"She's a good kid. So is Logan by the way. He takes good care of his little sister." He patted my knee and said, "You've done a fantastic job with them Tilda, despite everything you all have gone through."

We arrived at my house shortly after Cassie. Since she has a key, and she's a mom, so I found my crew already settled in with cartoons and cereal.

Cassie got up from the sofa.

"I'll see you guys in a bit. I'm stopping by Whole Foods to pick up some goodies for later! Michael! Jameson! Come on, we have to go!" Cassie shouted to the boys, who ran downstairs like wildebeests in the wild to follow her out the door. My wildebeests followed after them.

"Well my loves, I'm in desperate need of a shower. I'll return once I'm cleaned up. Deacon, help yourself to anything in the kitchen. We have tea and coffee pods in the cookie jar."

I decided on a relaxing bath since my muscles were beginning to ache already from my run. Lavender Epsom salts were exactly what I needed. It also gave me the opportunity to shamelessly hear the conversation downstairs.

"Mr. Deacon, where are you from?" Logan asked as he slurped his Frosted Flakes, dribbling sugary milk down his chin.

"I'm from Ireland. Have you heard of it?'

"Uh, yeah? I'm in 4th grade. I like maps. I draw the world a lot, too."

"The whole world? Well that's quite an accomplishment. Have you been to Ireland?"

"No. I've been to Epcot at Disneyworld. Is it like that?"

"Err, not quite. No, Ireland is beautiful with green hills and bustling cities full of excitement. I'm from a city that has huge medieval castles from long ago."

Logan's eyes widened. The mere idea of a town

that provided the image of medieval warfare perked his interest.

"Do you have battles there?"

"Yes, sir. They're called reenactments in fact. Men dress up like knights and battle it out, well pretend to. If you like, one day I'll take you there if you come visit."

"Mr. Deacon are you ever coming back here. To America?" Livia asked.

"I don't know. I hope so. I enjoy your family's company. Although, I wonder if George has decided if she likes me or not yet." George raised her head in response to hearing her name, saw there were no treats being offered and lay back down to her former comatose position.

"George likes everybody. Unless you're the grass cutter guys. She hates them. All she does is bark the whole time they're here. Super annoying." Logan said

I finished my lavender Epsom salt bath, dressed and headed downstairs. I could hear the kids chatting away with Deacon and it warmed my heart. It made me a bit sad though, since he was leaving tomorrow.

"Did you guys get something to eat?"

"Yes, but I'm still hungry. Can I have some peanut butter and bread?" Logan recently re-discovered peanut butter and it's now his go-to for every meal.

"Okay, Logan but you have to make it yourself." That's my other struggle. He's ten. He should be able to make his own sandwich, but despite his abilities, he still wants me to do it. I think it's a combination of laziness and not wanting to waste the peanut butter with a mess. He's not stellar at using the knife to spread yet.

The kids hung out in the living room, drawing and using their new (refurbished) Christmas iPads while Deacon and I sat on the sofa, drinking coffee and watching Food Network. I may have won a lottery of sorts however my kids are rough on electronics. Rough enough that I get them last year's models, which are pretty much the same the new models and are a fraction of the price, might I add. I supposed I learned a bit of Aunt Beebie's frugalness.

I knew this feeling of contentment would be short lived. Next Saturday I'd be sitting in the same spot, watching the kids play, listening to George snore and on the other side of me, would be an empty sofa cushion. I wouldn't have a warm arm around me. A sneaky kiss on my cheek when the kids weren't watching. I would be alone. Again.

We headed over to Cassie's house where she planned a brunch extravaganza in about two hours. She never ceases to amaze me. She likes to be the 'Hostess with the Mostest' which she wears proudly on her pink apron.

Cassie dinged her champagne glass and said, "I would like to make a toast to my brave friend who hates exercise but ventured out in the freezing cold this morning to finish her 5K. Another accomplishment can be marked off Aunt Beebie's Bucket List! Proud of ya, Tilda. Cheers."

I took a sip of my drink and realized I had another person to toast. "I'd like to also say cheers to my Aunt Beebie. Without her, I would still be in my pajamas on this late Saturday morning. I would also be about ten pounds heavier. Cheers Aunt Beebie!"

Everyone shouted in joyous union, "Cheers to Aunt Beebie!"

Cheers to my Aunt Beebie indeed.

Logan and Livia played with Cassie's kids in their playroom, Cassie was busy cleaning up her already clean and tidy kitchen, while Deacon and I cozied up on the sofa in front of the fire.

"Tilda, I just realized, I've never taken you out on a proper romantic date. Drinks at Brodie's or burgers at Shake Shack don't count."

"Deacon Kelly, any moment I spend with you is romantic. Especially if it includes listening to you play guitar and sing at Brodie's."

He kissed my hand and said, "Be that as it may, I'm leaving tomorrow, and I'd like to take you out somewhere nice. Would you indulge me? Cassie offered to let the kids sleep over here tonight."

"Well, you seem to have figured this all out. How can I say no?"

"I hope I made it difficult enough to." Deacon kissed me softly, leaving me with an ache in my stomach as his lips lingered.

"Well hello you two love birds. Is our plan on for

tonight, Deacon?"

"Yes Cassie, I believe it is."

"Is that okay with you, Tilda? My boys have been dying for a sleepover at our house. They have a plan upstairs for an indoor campout."

"My kids have been asking for the same thing. Ever since the night we went out and I met..." That was it. I'd held it in as long as I could. Maybe it was the fatigue from running. Maybe it was hormones. Maybe it was the realization that I had fallen head over heels for a man that was leaving me.

"Shhh. Don't cry, Tilda. I promise it's not forever." Deacon held me, rubbing my hair softly as I sobbed all over his black button-down shirt.

"I'm sorry."

"Don't be sorry. I'm sorry. I'm sorry you must go through this. I wouldn't be leaving if I didn't have to. I promise you Tilda."

"I know, Deacon."

I did know. I had complete faith in him despite not completely understanding it all. It didn't make me feel any better though.

We spent most of the afternoon together, until it was time to take the kids home. I needed to rest if I was going to spend the evening out and they needed to get cleaned up and pack for their sleepover.

"You guys are sure you're okay sleeping over all night at Ms. Cassie's house?"

Livia jumped up and down and screamed, "Yes! I'm so excited! Logan are you excited?"

"Yes." Logan replied, sitting on the floor, drawing his spacecraft with intense focus.

"Ms. Cassie is coming by to pick you guys up soon so be sure and finish up. She's taking you guys to the bounce house place before dinner.

"What?! That's awesome!" Logan exclaimed.

As the kids reveled in the joy of their upcoming bounce house visit, I went to pick out my outfit for my date. January is a tough month to look sexy and still be warm. I settled on some black jeans, black cashmere oversized sweater and wedge heeled boots.

"Mom! Ms. Cassie is here!" Logan shouted from downstairs.

"Okay! Let her in, Logan!"

I gathered Logan and Livia's sleepover things and helped Cassie get them in the car.

"Cassie, thank you so much for this. I can't believe this is my last night with Deacon."

"I know. But it's just temporary, Tilda. Don't worry. I have a good feeling about you guys."

I hoped she was right.

"Okay, guys. Give me hugs and I'll see you in the morning. I love you." I kissed Logan and Livia goodbye and wished Cassie luck. She assured me it would all be fine, the evening with four kids as well as my Deacon situation.

"Right, Tilda. I told myself. No more crying. You have makeup to finish." I resolved to enjoy my night. That included having perfectly blended makeup.

Once I finished getting ready, I poured myself a glass of wine to relax before Deacon arrived, who was right on time. I opened the door to see Deacon dressed impeccably. Perfectly tailored charcoal pants with a snug, white button shirt and houndstooth wool blazer. He always looked good, regardless of what he wore, but tonight's outfit was something special.

Deacon took my hand and announced, "Your chariot awaits you, milady."

He opened the car door for me, holding my hand while I got in.

"You look beautiful," he said as he kissing me, gently. "Are you sure you want to leave? We could always stay here and order in."

"Deacon! This was your idea!" I responded reproachfully.

"Was it? Damn." He winked at me and we drove off to our restaurant.

Deacon chose a dark and quiet Italian restaurant in a new, trendy part of town. It had been so long since I'd been to a romantic dinner, I actually felt nervous with a bit of excitement mixed in.

When I was married, my husband and I would occasionally go out. There came a point however, when candle lit dinners became few and far between. Dinners at home were more frequent with less romance and more French fries and other kid friendly fare.

"Tilda, what are you thinking about?" Deacon asked, pouring a glass of Prosecco for me as the soft music played in the background.

"Just how happy I am when I'm with you. I was anxious about going out tonight, yet once we sat down, I felt safe and calm. You make me feel calm, Deacon Kelly. I'm going to miss that."

"I feel the same way about you. You're the first woman I've been with that has her shit together. You don't play games. I love that about you, Tilda."

I laughed at the idea. "You think I have my shit together? Hah!"

"You do, trust me. My exes back home were jealous and possessive. I can work at the pub here and play my music and not worry you're going to beat up any lady that makes eyes at me."

I laughed at the thought and said, "Well just because I don't doesn't mean I don't want to." I did get kind of jealous, although I trusted Deacon for some reason. Despite my cheating husband.

I had a lovely butternut squash risotto, while Deacon opted for the salmon and bucatini. All paired nicely with the Prosecco Deacon chose for us.

After a delicious meal and dessert, Deacon drove me back home.

"Wait, you passed my street."

"I thought we could go back to my place. For old time's sake."

I hadn't been to Deacon's place, behind Cassie's house, since the morning after the first night we met.

Holding my hand, he led me into the guest

house. I paused for a moment, stunned. Deacon had lit candles everywhere.

"Don't worry, they're battery operated. I don't think Cass would like it if I burned her guest house down."

"No, I don't suppose she would. Deacon, this is so romantic."

"Alexa, play 'The Way You Look Tonight.'" The same song we danced to on Thanksgiving night. "Tilda, care to dance?"

"I'd love to," I whispered.

"Every memory of our time together is held in my heart. I want you to know, Tilda Loxley, that I will never forget any of it. I will use those memories to guide me back to you."

We danced to Tony Bennett slowly as he kissed me with tender passion and guided me to his bed where we did very little napping. Over and over again.

Chapter 9

Deacon had an early morning flight to Dublin, so I said my goodbye to him when he took me home. I didn't want Logan and Livia to see my devastation, so I kept my meltdowns private. My Irish fella promised me this wasn't a final goodbye. I hoped that was true, but my heart was in survival mode.

The best thing to keep from dwelling over a past love is to have an outrageous Bucket List from your deceased aunt. Trust me. It provides a whole new reason to stress and cry and basically question everything you thought you knew about yourself.

For example, I always thought of myself as a quick learner. I picked up new skills rather quickly when I was in school. However, that has not been the case for learning a new language.

Since Aunt Beebie didn't specify which foreign language to learn, I decided on Italian for my trip to Italy (that still needed to be planned.) I've read many Venetians do not identify with being Italian, but rather, Venetian. It appears to me though, if I want to order a glass of wine, I need to learn Italian.

While I muddled my way through this Bucket List, I sometimes wished I had Aunt Beebie to answer questions. Like, did she intend on learning a new language fluently? I doubted I could get by with only knowing how to ask for a glass of wine, but how much did I need know? Italians speak quite fast. Did she want to be able to speak Italian and discuss her opinion on European immigration? Or did she simply want to know how to order some gelato and get a taxi?

I resolved to do my best to learn as much as I could. Although, I couldn't see myself discussing European immigration in my own language, so I took that topic off the table. That made me think I should probably go back to listening to *The World* on NPR to learn more about European immigration and other thought-provoking topics.

I was still taking my dance class once a week, which I really enjoyed. My dance partner, Kyle finally proposed to his girlfriend. Thankfully, she said yes. Kyle decided to continue taking dance classes with me. His fiancée had no objections, probably because she didn't find a romantic threat. To be clear, I didn't have any concerns either. Kyle was extremely adorable, but despite his age, he looked about 20, perspired like a beast in the Amazon and reminded of a skinnier version of my cousin Billy, who I hadn't seen in about 20 years, since he became a missionary in South America, or was it South Africa? Either way, I did not have any lustful thoughts for dear, Kyle.

As January flew by, Valentine's Day did as well. Another lonely day that is filled with Mexican takeout. Deacon sent me flowers and we had a Facetime conversation. The kids enjoyed being able to talk to him and see his face. I did as well, but

I still missed him something awful. We planned a trip in April for Venice and I absolutely could not wait. Deacon insisted on organizing and paying for his own flight accommodations although he agreed, since I was more particular regarding suitable hotels, I would handle that portion of our trip. I was excited about Venice and knowing we would reunite soon.

As we exited February, March roared in and I had other items on my Bucket List to focus on. Specifically, my trip to see the Northern Lights. I'd chosen March for our trip as Logan and Livia would have an entire week off school for Spring Break. They weren't excited about spending a week in Alaska, so I compromised on three days.

I had seen photos of the magnificent Aurora Borealis but never would have imagined taking the long trek for an in-person view. I also never imagined I would bring my two kids. Nevertheless, here we were in Alaska, the night before our early wake up call.

Livia wasn't interested in what she was about to see tomorrow morning. She was rather upset that we couldn't access Nickelodeon on the hotel television. No amount of education regarding the breathtaking lights could pique her interest.

Logan, on the other hand, was so excited he could barely contain himself. While Livia so far has been a child with a vivid imagination, creating extremely detailed storylines for her stuffed animals, Logan was my curious child. At the age of two, he could tell me every planet in our solar system, in order, simply from watching a cartoon on the Disney Channel. When I was two, I am certain the exclusion of Pluto from the planets was the furthest thing from my mind. I just wanted to know if I could eat ice cream for dinner and watch Sesame Street.

Fortunately, I was able to get both kids to sleep. Unfortunately, for said kids to have the amount of sleep required to prevent extreme moodiness, I had needed to get them asleep about five hours earlier.

The alarm on my phone went off and unfortunately, only woke me up.

I whispered to the kids, “It’s time to get up, guys.”

“I don’t wanna get up! I’m cold!” Livia whined from underneath her warm comforter when I woke her. To be clear, I did not make my children sleep in an Alaskan igloo. We were in an ample sized, rather toasty 4-star hotel room.

“Livia! Stop yelling in my ear! I’m trying to sleep!” Logan fussed from the other side of the warm comforter. I assumed a two-bed queen size room would have plenty of room for the two of them, but Livia likes to snuggle. This meant poor Logan had her whiny, morning breath all up in his personal space.

Livia ignored Logan’s request and said, “I’m tired! I don’t wanna go to the Roaroara Boralallis!”

Logan, having none of this mispronunciation,

groaned, "Livia. It's Aurora Borealis! We have to get up if we want to see it. Which we don't."

"What?!" I squealed loud enough for my shared-wall neighbors to hear. I doubted their stay in Anchorage included this rare adventure but sure they were now awake for it, regardless.

"I'm tired! Let's do it another day." Logan rolled over to continue his slumber.

I was feeling defeated. Logan is my ringer. I knew he was excited, and I counted on him to build Livia's excitement. This was an absolute disaster.

"Get up. Get up!!!! We have a bus to catch in 20 minutes. I don't care if you have to go in your pajamas. We are getting on that bus and we're going to see the Roarroara Borallalis!!!!

The kids paused, possibly in shock, looked at each other, picked up their clothes and got dressed.

The bus ride to our prime viewing location was just under two hours. Specific routes were adjusted as the bus driver and trip leader learned of possible sightings. The kids stole a few more winks of sleep while I enjoyed the quiet with my Yeti coffee cup full of, you guessed it, hot coffee.

It was mostly older travelers, perhaps working on their own Bucket List. I saw one group of women on what appeared to be a girl's trip. One man, sitting across from me was traveling on his own, with a rather fancy looking camera hanging from his neck.

"Is this your first time to see the lights?" I whispered to him, to not disturb the sleeping cubs.

The solo man, quietly chuckled, "Well, it's actually my second trip and hopefully the first time."

"What do you mean?" I asked, confused.

"I was on this bus two days ago. We all waited, but the lights didn't want to put a show on for us that morning."

"What?" I simply said. I had 3 plane tickets for tomorrow morning to get us out of this beautiful, although, extremely cold place.

"Didn't you read the brochure? There's no guarantee you'll actually see the Northern Lights."

"No guarantee? I guess I forgot that part." Now that he mentioned it, I did remember reading something about that. I didn't really take it seriously back when I was in pre-planning stages.

I started to panic. If my kids knew there may not be a show to make up for their early morning wake up call, I was in big trouble. Not to mention, I wouldn't be able to check this off Aunt Beebie's Bucket List! I couldn't make this trip again! I simply didn't have time.

"Are you okay? You seem a bit pale."

"I can't breathe. I think I'm having a panic attack. Tell me a story. Something that isn't about ruining my life in a completely superficial way. Go."

The man stuttered in his own state of possible panic.

"Once, on a work trip to Rome, I was trying to take a photo of the Trevi Fountain and while maneuvering around a group of Chinese tourists, I fell in the fountain, taking an old lady with me. The Carabinieri came out of nowhere and for a moment, I was on Italy's most hated list. My broken Italian and press credentials helped explain the embarrassing accident, so they didn't arrest me. Thank god. It did make me wonder what prisoners eat in an Italian prison though. Do you think Italian food? Like, pasta? Parmigiano Reggiano sticks like you get in McDonald's Happy Meals?"

His story was so crazy I immediately forgot everything and burst into hysterical laughter.

"Is that true or did you make it up on the spot?"

The man held up one hand and swore, "On my Grandma Ruthie's life, I promise it's all true."

"Wow. That's some adventure. Do they really put sticks of cheese in the McDonald's Happy Meals? That's true?" It sounded fabulous. Another reason to visit Italy. Cheese.

"Sure is. My son came with me on a trip once. I don't typically purchase Happy Meals."

"You have a son? How old is he?"

"Well, now he's 14 and way too cool for Happy Meals or trips with his father. He lives with my ex-wife and her new husband in Chicago. It's amicable but my wife's husband is a jerk. Super nice, handsome and makes twice what I do. I think his 401K is more productive too."

I laughed at his humor and the idea he thought another man was more handsome than he was. I thought he was quite attractive. He had dark wavy hair and warm brown eyes. A friendly and kind face, even with the need to shave. Being up in the middle of the night, I don't think I would have shaved either.

"I'm Tilda, by the way."

The handsome stranger reached his hand out to shake and said, "Sam. Nice to meet you, Tilda. I have to say, I'm rather impressed you brought your kids on this trip."

"Well, I'm a single mom on a mission. Sometimes that means bringing the kids along for the journey. They'll forgive me one day."

"I'm sure they will. And don't worry. I hear it's a 50/50 chance of seeing the lights, so my failed trip increases your odds considerably." He took a sip of his tea and asked, "So why the Northern Lights?"

"Well, I suppose you told me a story. So now it's my turn. My Aunt Beebie passed away and left me her Bucket List to finish. This is on it and so here I am. In Alaska because Iceland was just too far away, and I don't have passports for the kids yet."

"A Bucket List? That's awesome. So where are you at on it? Is there a lot to do?" He seemed genuinely excited about my story.

I pulled out my rumpled sheet of paper. I always kept it with me, and it was beginning to look like it.

"Hmm. Let's see what's left. I haven't evaluated it recently. Here we are:

1. Fly in a hot air balloon- Not too excited for that one. I mean, what if I fall out? Can that happen? Yikes.

2. Learn a new language- I'm working on that. I can order wine now in Italian.
3. Take a gondola ride in Venice- Planning my trip. Hence the wine ordering in Italian.
4. Sleep overnight in a haunted house- Need to work on that. Don't really know any haunted houses.
5. Learn to dance- Still working on that. I can successfully do the waltz though.
6. Pose nude for an art class- Ugh. Never want to do that.
7. See the Northern Lights- Let's hope they come out.
8. Teach a class- Have no idea. I don't think I know enough of anything to competently teach a class.

"There we are. I actually have a lot more to do than I thought."

"Lucky for you, I'm a world traveler. Care for some advice?"

"Sure."

"The gondola rides and water taxis are expensive. Plan to pay about 80 euros for them. If you're claustrophobic, take a Xanax before exploring the city. Tight streets and a bazillion tourists make it difficult to get anywhere."

"You don't seem to like Venice."

"No, I do. It's a beautiful city. I just wish it had a lot less people. I do recommend visiting the small islands. Less tourists."

"Okay, advice noted. What else have ya got?" I asked my new acquaintance, who seemed to be a wealth of travel information.

"Have you been to Louisiana before? There's a plantation home called "The Grande Oaks" said to be one of the most haunted places in the country. It's a beautiful hotel tucked away in a small town. St. Francisville, I believe. Anyway, it's worth it for the culture even if you don't see any ghosts."

It sounded like a perfect getaway for Cassie and me. And maybe even Tabitha.

The two-hour journey passed quickly, thanks to my conversation with Sam. The kids woke up when the bus came to a stop. Their nap seemed to help their demeanor somewhat. I handed them each a small bottle of water and a breakfast bar to prevent starvation and preserve the newly positive attitude. I needed to be prepared if this trip went to the toilet.

The tour guide stood up to let us know we were ready to leave the bus. Everyone stirred in eager anticipation. I think the kids were even excited at this point. I was still nervous as I had Sam's 50/50 comment whirling around in my head, I was still nervous.

The group exited the bus and looked for a good place for the viewing. Professional looking people set up their cameras and tripods, while the rest of us just looked around and waited. It was bitterly cold, but our winter gear gave us the warmth we needed.

The tour guide motioned us over to them and said, “We’ve been told there’s been some sightings of lights around this viewing location. So now, we wait folks. Audrey will pass out warm beverages for you.”

Audrey, we were told earlier was the tour guide’s daughter, home from a college break. She poured the hot drinks from two portable urns. One provided coffee, the other hot chocolate. I noticed the group of ladies pull out a small bottle of Baileys to top off their cocoa drinks.

The kids had hot chocolate, while I stuck with the coffee. It’s astonishing how quickly a beverage can cool off in the frigid Alaskan temperatures. I was thankful I invested in quality outdoor wear. The Northern Lights are not for anyone who does not like cold weather.

“Mama, when are the lights coming out? I’m tired.” Logan asked jumping up and down. Possibly out of boredom. Possibly for survival. It was so freaking cold. If we didn’t see any lights, my kids were going to report me for child abuse. I could hear it now. *Ma’am you forced your kids to stand outside in the frigid temperatures for over two hours. You are a terrible mother. Give her the maximum penalty.*

“We have to wait, Logan. Mother Nature sticks to her own schedule. Which is no schedule.” I looked down at my phone to see if I still had no signal.

Suddenly Livia squealed so loud I dropped my

phone in the frozen wilderness.

"Mommy!! Look!! It's the Roara Boarallalis!"

And there it was. It was breathtaking.

In the distance, we saw a fluid looking stream of green that grew in intensity as it travelled across the sky. All feelings of cold disappeared. We stood there, entranced. I could feel a single tear stream down my face. This was the most beautiful thing I had ever seen.

I looked over to see Logan and Livia as they watched in awe. Any misgivings about taking them on this trip disappeared. My two amazing kids had just witnessed something some people will only dream about. In fact, a year ago, I never would have even dreamed about it. This was all thanks to Aunt Beebie.

As the lights danced across the Alaskan sky, it felt as though my aunt was in there, taking a break from Heaven to see how we were. I remembered as a child, when we would dance elegantly in her living room with her colorful, eccentric scarves. Neither of us had any dance training, yet we glided across her wood floors as though we were Ginger Rogers.

I could hear photographers snapping photos, people taking deep breaths out of sheer amazement. Sam, my seat neighbor was no exception. He looked over for a second, smiled with a nod and returned to his photography. I didn't know any of these people, yet in this moment we all shared the same unforgettable experience.

We all met the magical Aurora Borealis.

Chapter 10

I had two weeks until my Italian adventure. Logan and Livia were staying back since school was still in session. They missed a day during our Alaska trip and although the sheer thought of being away from them for an entire week made my stomach churn, I knew they would be in good hands. I was leaving on a Thursday night. The kids' grandmother offered to stay with the kids until Monday and they would be with Cassie the rest of the week.

In preparation, I decided to try and speak all the Italian I'd learned so far, every day. In the morning, when the kids got up, I would announce, *Buongiorno*! When I dropped them off in carpool I'd say, *Ciao!* And at pickup I would ask, *Come stata la tua giornata?* I'd worked really hard to learn that phrase. In response, the kids would say, *bene*, which meant good.

"Ah, *bene*. But really, how was your day?"

"*Bene*." Logan replied.

"I know, but you don't have to reply in Italian now. I just want to know really how your day was?"

Logan, grunted with annoyance and said louder, "*Bene*! My day was *bene*!"

"Okay. Got it. How was your day, Liv? Was your day *bene* as well?"

"My day was *fantastica*!" My slightly more positive and happier child wanted to learn new words beyond good. Last night she asked what fantastic was in Italian and so we now have *fantastica*.

I would hardly say I'd learned my new language, but it was coming along. I was rather impressed with myself, considering I'm a 40-year old who sometimes forgets what year her kids were born.

As the days passed and I continued my Italian conversation attempts, I maniacally planned for my absence. Several grocery shopping trips, print-outs of every possible necessary contact from the pediatrician to recently retired preschool teachers, I finally felt confident I could leave the continent, and everything would be A-Okay in the event of an emergency. I even left a message for my vet to let them know I was leaving the country, just in case George had any emergencies while in Cassie's or my mother-in-law's care.

Deacon planned on meeting me in Venice Sunday evening. While I still had not created my own Bucket List, I had always wanted to see The Leaning Tower of Pisa. To do this, I chose to fly into Pisa and take a train to Venice. According to the schedule, it was a few hours but a wonderful way of seeing the Italian countryside.

I knew I should pack light. However, given the fact I was going to be in one of the most fashionable countries in the world, there was no way I'd accomplish that feat. So, one long shopping trip, giant suitcase and overstuffed carry-on bag later I was on my way to Pisa.

The first leg of my flight was delayed about 40

minutes, which meant getting to my second flight was damn near impossible.

Flying into London Heathrow meant I had to go through customs and security before having access to my gate. A weary traveler once said: *Walking through London Heathrow is possibly akin to several of Dante's Circles of Hell.* The weary traveler was me, Tilda Loxley.

There were so many people in the airport, rushing to my gate was extremely difficult. Dragging my wheeled carry-on bag behind me, I ran over people's toes, (apologizing profusely in passing); held in every ounce of pee (I didn't have time to stop at the restroom) and ignored a plethora of luxury shops along the way (I didn't have time to shop.)

As it turned out, my boarding agents knew I was late and held up the plane departure for me. I showed them my boarding pass, passport and they practically shoved me into the tunnel to my plane.

I was extremely thankful I shelled out the extra money for first class. It saved me from a walk of shame through the multiple rows of seats even though it wasn't my fault my plane was delayed, or that security took forever because some dummy accidentally left a gun or knife or something in their carry-on bag.

The flight to Galileo Galilei Airport from Heathrow was quick. Because it was a small airport, customs and baggage claim was much easier than Heathrow. This weary traveler was still quite weary and ready to find her lodging.

As I waited in the taxi line, I marveled at the façade of the airport. It was covered in green shrubbery with the Galilei International Airport sign on top. There was outdoor bistro seating and a lush green lawn where people could sit, relax and enjoy the art sculptures. Never in my life had I been to such a beautiful airport. I immediately felt *La Dolce Vita*.

It was a quick taxi ride to my hotel, albeit treacherous. As the driver maneuvered through tiny streets, avoiding pedestrians and other cars, I began to feel queasy. Once we reached my hotel, I was elated to step out of the car and pay my fare.

I reached into my purse and pulled out my VISA card when the taxi driver promptly said, "No. No credit card. Only cash." The driver pointed me to the conveniently located ATM machine next to the hotel. I assumed all taxis accepted credit cards nowadays, but this driver was adamant. Who was I to question an Italian taxi driver?

I nervously approached the ATM and worried I wouldn't know how to use it, being that I was in Italy and everything was in Italian. Thankfully, the taxi driver helped me figure it all out and accepted his cash and tip with a proper *grazie*. A new customer dragged their bags to his car, and he was off, presumably on another speedy airport adventure.

My hotel, although glamorous from the lobby photos, was rather minimal. My pillows were flat, the bedding was plain but there was a nice television with cartoons in Italian. I decided to sit and relax for a bit with my familiar cartoons until I figured out my next plan of action. However, watching Peppa Pig made me miss my kids desperately. I wanted to Facetime with them, but realized it was still early in the U.S. and they would still be in school.

Once I decided Peppa was not going to help my emotional state, I ventured outside for a walk. The street outside of the hotel was bustling with tourists, people riding bikes, horse-drawn carriages and a lot of outdoor restaurants. It was everything I wanted and more.

Thanks to my Rick Steves travel book about Tuscany, I knew Italians ate dinner much later than Americans. Since it was only 6:00 pm, some dinner spots had yet to open. To my right, I could see the magnificent Leaning Tower of Pisa. The sun had begun to set, and the lights shone on it as though it were from the heavens. It was breathtaking to see something with so much history and beauty. As a kid I never would have dreamed I would actually get to see the same sights I read about in my history books. While Aunt Beebie did her share of travel, my family didn't really travel much outside of the United States. We did the Disney trips, and a National Park or two but once my father got sick, vacations were few and far between. Once he passed away, my mother was busy working and being a single mother. Vacations were a luxury that we didn't have the time or money to enjoy. I think that's why I was determined to make the most of this trip.

It was getting too late to explore the walls around the city, so I headed back down the main street near the hotel. I was hesitant to eat somewhere too close to the Tower fearing it was too touristy. I was also somewhat hesitant to explore too much on my own, not really knowing the city. I kept walking though, past the hotel and some souvenir shops to a cute little restaurant, called Pepperoncino. There were a couple of people eating inside but the tables outside were nearly full, even at 6:30 pm. I thought this must be a good sign.

"*Ciao*! You need a table?" The older, bald man asked me as I approached the restaurant.

I decided to practice my limited Italian.

"*Si. 1 persona. Per favore*?"

"Okay. Come sit." He handed me the menu as well as the wine list. I couldn't wait to have some Italian wine.

"*Vino Bianco?* Per favore?"

"A glass or ½ liter?" He asked in English. He was probably getting annoyed with my feeble attempts at his native language, he didn't show it though. The man, who may have been the owner or manager, was friendly and patient.

"Oooh, ½ liter please!" I wasn't driving. I could see my hotel from the table.

The cheerful, balding man brought out my wine and took my dinner order. I have a habit of wanting to order everything on the menu of a new restaurant because I want to try more than one thing. I chose to only order a few items though. The unfortunate part of sitting alone at dinner is you have nobody to blame the gluttony on but yourself.

While I sipped my wine and nibbled at my fried zucchini blossoms, I thought how strangely comfortable it was to be sitting alone. When I was married, I relied on my husband for nearly everything. That included emotional support and dinner conversation. When he died, the kids would eat with me or more typical, I would just order delivery.

"Ah *signora*, I have your Spaghetti Pomodoro and a side of parmesan. Would you like more wine?"

"It looks delicious. No, I think this was enough. Well, I don't know. Maybe a glass of prosecco? It is my first ever night in Italy."

"Your first night? What brings you to Pisa?"

I wasn't sure how a bucket list would translate so I simply said, "I have a list of places and things I want to do and one of them was to see your Leaning Tower. It's *bellissima* by the way."

The man smiled and said, "A bucket list? Very nice. Okay, enjoy dinner, *Signora*." He patted me on the shoulder and attended his other patrons who all seemed very happy as well.

I couldn't wait to dig into my spaghetti. It was a simple dish yet when made with the love and the right ingredients, filled my heart with joy. I dipped the tiny spoon into the small metal bowl of parmesan, sprinkled it across my plate of pasta and then twirled the delicate combination of tomato sauce and spaghetti into my fork...

"Oh my god this is divine!" I said, rather loudly. I couldn't help it. The couple next to me laughed and nodded their heads in agreement.

"Sorry, my first pasta in Italy." As well as my third glass of wine? To be honest, I had no idea how much wine a ½ liter really was. I was too busy enjoying it.

They smiled at me and went back to whatever discussion they were having. The feeling here was so incredibly different. People seemed to enjoy themselves. They weren't sitting on their phones, idly scrolling through other people's Instagram photos. They didn't bother themselves with judgement of other people or worry about others judging them. They just lived.

I finished my dinner, deciding to not have dessert. Since the streets were still busy and lively, even well after dark, so I chose to walk around a bit to let my food settle. There were men selling light up toys for children, a musician playing what sounded like the theme to Game of Thrones, and families walking to dinner.

I wanted to talk to Deacon but settled on a text. Since returning to Ireland, he took his job back at the pub he worked at before, which meant this was work time for him.

In Pisa. It's amazing. Can't wait to see u.

Can't wait to see u. Ciao, Deacon.

I was still too full for dessert until, I found a gelateria close to the hotel. Again, probably to the dismay of the Italian lady who spoke wonderful English, I chose to try and order in Italian.

"*Un piccolo gelato per favore*?"

"A small? Yes, *cono* or *coppeta*?" She asked.

Cono sounded a lot like cone, which I noticed most people around me selected, so I took chance on my assumption and said, "*Cono*, please."

It was all rather overwhelming. There were the obvious flavors, chocolate, vanilla etc. although others I wasn't sure about.

"Is that a chocolate hazelnut?"

"*Si, Bacio*."

"Okay. I'd like that. Wait, *Vorrie, un gelato bacio*."

"What else?" The lady asked, quickly.

I was confused for a moment then I realized she was asking if I wanted another scoop of something else. I didn't want another scoop, but I got nervous, so I just asked for chocolate.

If you give a girl a lot of wine, and then give a girl multiple scoops of gelato on a cone, that girl might eat all her gelato without dropping the top scoop on the ground.

Sadly, I was not that girl.

I made it back to my hotel room safely and spoke with Logan and Livia about their day. My mother-in-law had taken them for ice cream after school.

"Well how about that? We were probably having ice cream together at the same time and we didn't even know it."

"But you had gelato?" Logan asked.

"Yep and it was delicious."

"Have you seen the Leaning Tower of Pisa yet?"

"I have! I've taken some photos, so I'll send them to Grandma okay?" I sighed, holding back tears and said to them, "I wish you were here. I miss you." I was still a bit drunk and hoped it wasn't obvious.

"We miss you too! Okay we have to go. Grandma is taking us out to dinner later. Bye!" Both kids shouted into the phone, then hung up. They seemed to be dealing with the short separation much better than me.

I was exhausted from the long travel, jet lag and sight-seeing. It was definitely time for bed.

Bed lasted much longer than I thought. I planned on getting the complimentary breakfast in the morning but missed it. In fact, I missed lunch as well. I woke to someone knocking at my door at...2:15 pm?! I slept until 2:15 pm in the afternoon?!

It was probably housekeeping. I scrambled out of bed, hoping they didn't have to come in since I hadn't even brushed my teeth yet, let alone showered and dressed.

I unbolted the locks and opened the door. Expecting a hotel employee, I was shocked to find someone else.

"Deacon! What are you doing here?" I asked, trying to smooth my messy, slept on hair.

"Surprise!" We hugged and he gave me a sweet kiss on the cheek. He likely knew I had not brushed my teeth as well.

"What are you doing here? I thought you couldn't make it until Venice?" Part of me was annoyed that he was infringing on my solo adventure in Pisa, although the other part of me was elated because after one night, I was beginning to feel lonely.

"I pulled some favors and was able to get a few extra days off. It helps when your mum and dad are your boss."

"Your parents own the pub you work at?"

"Yeah, didn't I tell you that? It's been in the Kelly family over a hundred years."

"No, you haven't really told me much about your family at all." Which was true. I also had not asked which made me wonder if I was too self-absorbed, or he didn't want to talk about it.

"Not much to tell really. My dad, his dad and all the dads before have taken care of the pub, they expect me to as well. It's part of our family pride."

"So, your destiny has been chosen from the moment you were born?"

"Yep, pretty much. It made me a popular lad in school, but it wasn't what I dreamed of."

"I'm sorry. What did you dream of?"

"I wanted to be a footballer or a musician. Pipe dreams, really. How about you get yourself together and we go for a stroll. I need to see Pisa."

Deacon seemed eager to change the subject and

given this was his first time really opening up to me, I didn't want to push him. I also really needed to get cleaned up. I hadn't showered for an embarrassing amount of time.

Once I cleaned up and got dressed, we took to the streets of Pisa. We walked over to the tower first, because that obviously was Pisa's main attraction. Most of the day tourists had left Pisa last night, today a new set of tour groups, families and students arrived to get the obligatory photo with the beautiful piece of history.

I was eager to see more of Pisa. So far, it had welcomed me with open arms, and I knew there was more to Pisa than its star attraction.

A couple of side streets took us to the Piazza de Cavalieri, a piazza surrounded by stone buildings, one being an entrance to a university. The shocking thing was as the pedestrians strolled through the piazza, so did cars and trucks. It was a free for all, with tiny European cars maneuvering to avoid tourists and tourists ignoring the horns to avoiding meeting immediate death.

We made it through our personal Frogger experience to a small street that, again, allowed pedestrians and automobiles. Thankfully, the street was big enough to allow us to hug with the graffitied walls as the cars whizzed by with determination.

I was starving and needed some sustenance after our perilous stroll. I could smell pizza from a nearby spot, but we opted for what appeared to be a popular people watching restaurant.

An elderly man dressed in the finest linens held court with his people at a nearby table. I didn't know what he was saying but the people he sat with held onto his words as though he were the messiah himself. He wore a fir green suit with shiny gold cufflinks. His multi-color silk scarf wrapped effortlessly around his aging neck and white collared shirt. My attention couldn't be taken away however, from the multiple watches he wore as an accessory on his arm. I was fascinated by him and I think he noticed because for a moment, mid conversation, he paused and warmly smiled at me.

"So, my dear Tilda, are you going to have coffee or a drink? This is breakfast for you, yeah?" Deacon winked. "What are you looking at?" His back was turned to the fascinating old man thus missing a truly grand display.

"Don't look, but there's a man at the table back there. He's absolutely divine. You'll know when you see him. Don't look! He'll know we're talking about him."

"How can I see him then if I don't turn around and look?" Deacon asked, exasperated, wanting to see what my fuss was about.

"Go walk up to the window and pretend to look at the desserts. You'll see him when you walk back to the table."

Deacon did as I advised and as he casually walked back to our table, he gave the old man in the green suit a nod, acknowledging the jig was up and we were obviously checking him out.

"Did he see you? Why did you nod at him?"

"Because he nodded to me! He's a rather eccentric looking man. I imagine nosy tourists like us do this all the time." Deacon laughed and went back to his coffee vs alcohol dilemma. He smiled over the menu and said, "Okay I'm going to have a drink because it's not breakfast time for me."

"Fair enough." When the busy waiter finally came over to our table, I ordered a cappuccino and almond croissant, Deacon ordered his aperitif, AKA Guiness.

We sat and talked amongst the wafts of cigarette smoke from neighboring tables for a couple of hours. When the shops started opening back up from their siesta, we paid our bill to continue our stroll past them.

We walked down the Borgo Stretto and saw an abundance of shops. A toy store across from the café had just unlocked its doors. I was eager to pick up some Italian toys. It was so rare to see small, privately owned toy stores in the U.S. now. It reminded me of a beachside toy store I visited as a child on a family vacation. My mother let me have a horse marionette that I named Jingles. There were a lot of memories with that horse, untangling his strings, only to tangle them up more. It's hard to find toys like that in a Walmart toy aisle.

"Do you mind if I pick something up for Logan and Livia? Have they forgotten about me already?"

"Are you kidding? Livia talks about you every single day and Logan hasn't stopped asking me when we're going to Swords Castle. I think you made an impression on them."

"Ah that reminds me! I brought this for Logan." From out of his travel backpack, Deacon pulled out a small, pewter replica of what looked like Swords Castle.

It warmed my heart. Not only did he remember the conversation he had with my sweet boy, he brought him something to acknowledge it.

I gave Deacon a kiss. "He will love it. I can't wait to give it to him."

Logan was such a bright boy. His love of architecture began at a young age. He would draw world landmarks with great intricacy all day. At the age of four, I would participate in *how to draws* where my boy tried to teach his inept mother how to draw buildings like the Burj Khalifa and Tai Pei 101.

We continued our journey down the Borgo Stretto and crossed a bridge that took us to another set of shopping and food. The Corso Italia was just as marvelous. Where the previous street displayed smaller, local shops, the Corso boasted the standard H&M and Zara. This wasn't your ordinary chain store though. This H&M had beautiful marble staircases and Renaissance art.

Pisa was a city I resolved to be unappreciated. While day-trippers rushed to the tower for their photos and long walks up to the top, there was the rest of Pisa to explore. Food, that once off the beaten path tasted of love. Piazzas and museums that could rival some in Florence. But mostly, the Pisans were what left me with the biggest impression. They loved their city, their food and most importantly, their lives.

If this small Italian town was just a glimpse of what was in store for me, I couldn't wait to see Venice.

Chapter 11

After a night of pizza and a few carafes of wine, with plenty of romance, Deacon and I woke up relaxed and ready for our train to Venice. The train station was on the other side of the Corso Italia. From our hotel, it was about a 20-minute walk to the train station. It also meant we would be wheeling our bags through the city. Since it was our last day in Pisa, we wanted to take in as much as we could. In true Italian fashion, we ordered take away sandwiches and Cokes from the panini place across from the hotel. I was thankful we did because the food area in the train station was packed full of people and minus the quality and love of our bistro sandwiches.

We had a quick train transfer in Florence from Pisa, and I felt with some regret that I didn't schedule our train tickets differently so we could spend some time there. I didn't change the tickets though because where the regional train came every 20 minutes with a first come first serve seating arrangement, the Venice train was first class and designated seating, per my ticket. I was really growing to love first class.

We had to roll our suitcases quickly through the masses as our Venice train was on the exact opposite side of the Pisa train. Deacon, being the gentleman, grabbed my heavy and overpacked suitcase while I trailed behind with my handbag. I am all for women's equality but in this case, his muscles won.

Once we traveled through about five train cars, asked about three people if this was first class, then asked two people why they were in our seats, we finally sat down. I was happy to be able to relax for the next few hours. Being a typical tourist was exhausting.

"I've missed you, Tilda." Deacon held my hand as we snuggled in the train seats. I felt like a teenager. I had missed him too. "How's your list coming along? Done that naked art class yet?"

"Oh my god, no. It's last on my list. The rest is coming along. I'm planning my girl's trip to a haunted house. I've talked Cassie and my former arch nemesis, Tabitha, into joining me. We leave a few days after school is out. That way Logan and Livia can stay with their grandparents for the weekend while I'm gone."

"Former arch nemesis huh? Sounds interesting. Can't wait to meet her. Where is it? The haunted house?"

"It's called The Grande Oaks, in Louisiana. A guy I met on our Northern Lights trip told me about it. I've done some research and I think it's legit. There is a lot of history at an old plantation like that."

"I imagine there is. Well, you seem to be coming along quite well. Your aunt would be proud. So, tell me more about this guy you met on your Northern Lights trip."

"Deacon Kelly, are you jealous?"

"Yep."

"Well that's an honest answer. I don't think I was expecting that."

"Tilda, you are a beautiful woman with unbelievable magnetism."

I nearly choked on my sandwich. Me? Electric Magnetism?

"That's ridiculous, Deacon."

"It's true! I was drawn to you the moment I met you that night in Brodie's."

"That's because I literally wouldn't let you go. Do I need to remind you I forced myself onto you?"

"Oh Tilda. You didn't force anything on me. Those kisses were quite appreciated."

After nearly six months of whatever this was, I still blushed at his flirtation. I wanted to devour him right there on the train. I just kissed him on the cheek instead.

Our train took us through several beautiful Italian cities but once we saw the sparkling blue water surrounding us as our train glided next to it. There are a few times I've had this breath gasping moments. Landing into LaGuardia for my first NYC visit with a view of the bridges into Manhattan was one. This was another.

I felt excited, like a child looking out the window at night, hoping to sneak a peek of Santa and his reindeer. I glanced over at Deacon. He had the same expression.

When the train arrived at *Stazione di Venezia Santa Lucia,* we hurriedly gathered our bags to begin our Venetian adventure.

Deacon and I maneuvered out of the glamorous and very busy train station to find a water taxi. I remembered Sam at the Aurora Borealis telling me they were rather pricey. I wanted to experience the ultimate Venice though. Chances were high that I might never return, and I did have Aunt Beebie's money.

"Let's head over to the water taxi line. I think I'd rather do that. The water bus looks rather busy."

It is a strange feeling being somewhere that has zero cars. Every single form of transportation is water based in Venice. It also means that you will occasionally get splashed by water. Mascara users should heed my advice and wear waterproof mascara unless you want to look like a female character from a horror movie, like I did.

Thankfully, I am a well-prepared tourist. Being a mom trains a person for any possible scenario. I had every type of wipe needed for every type of situation. Sanitary, antibacterial, speedy makeup removal, you name it and I had it.

Deacon of course, thought this whole experience was hilarious. Once I no longer had mascara running down my face, so did I. Having black makeup drizzle down your face takes away any preconceived notion that this will be a glamorous vacation and that you are like Jennifer Aniston or some other fabulous movie star.

Our water taxi dropped us off right next to our Airbnb. I thought it would be nice to have a homey stay with Deacon. This was our first real getaway together...alone... sharing one bathroom. Very intimate. Again, I'm a well-prepared traveler, which meant I packed a couple bottles of Poo-Pourri.

Our apartment was cozy, clean and well decorated. Our host stocked the kitchen with coffee capsules to use with the Nespresso machine. She had small packages of breakfast cookies and sugar set to the side in a cute decorative bowl. The refrigerator was sparse but that was to be expected. She did include a few liters of bottled water though.

"Since it's a bit late for museums so what do you say we take a walk down our street and just explore? I think there is a grocery store down the way according to the host's manual."

"Absolutely, but first can I do this?" Deacon wrapped his arms around me and gave a passionate kiss. We still had a lot of kissing to catch up on, apparently.

"Oh! I forgot to tell you!" I said mid-kiss. "My dance class is going to have a dance recital! We're going to wear proper dance costumes! Like Dancing with the Stars!"

I was very excited about the dance costumes. When you become a grownup, you can't dress up like however you want. Livia could put on her Princess Anna dress and go ride her bike and nobody would think otherwise. If I did that someone would call the authorities on me.

"I hope I can come, Tilda. That sounds spectacular. When is it?"

"I don't remember the date. It isn't for a while. Maybe September? You'll have time to sort your life out by then. But for now, I can show you some of my other moves." I took Deacon's hand and led him to the bedroom. We were in one of the most romantic cities in the world and I had every intention of enjoying our time together.

A bit later, and much hungrier, we got dressed and walked down to the grocery store. The narrow supermarket had multiple aisles filled with fresh breads, cheeses, and every other staple one might need for their home. The store itself was too small to be burdened with large grocery carts, but they did provide medium-sized baskets with wheels that could be rolled throughout the store with minimal ankle bruising.

I liked the idea of going to the grocery store and just picking up what you needed. I probably have cans of vegetables and frozen chicken breasts that have been stored for several months. Why don't I just use it? Why did I buy it in the first place? This Venice trip is providing thought provoking introspection on the necessity of my Costco membership.

"Do you think people judge our age difference?" I asked as we carried our grocery bags down the street to the apartment.

"What people? I haven't seen anybody I know here yet."

"You know what I mean, Deacon. I'm obviously much older than you."

"It's not obvious at all. When I have a two-day scruff, I look at least 30. You on the other hand do not look a day over 35. That gives us a mere, few years age difference. Besides Tilda, it's nobody's fucking business." Deacon said casually, but matter of fact.

"You're right. It is none of their fucking business. Whoever they might be." If my hands weren't full of grocery bags, I would've grabbed his hand. Or butt. His butt was rather cute.

We walked up the several flights of stairs in our standard, no elevator Venetian building. I must say, I huffed and puffed more than Deacon, who's muscular legs and abs indicated he exercises more than I do. However, thanks to Aunt Beebie, I've also gotten in better shape. Six months ago, I may have had a coronary episode at the top of these steep stairs.

All this exercise was making me hungrier.

"Do you want to try that place we passed on the way back from the supermarket? It looked like it was getting busy. The host's manual recommends it."

"I will do whatever you want. I'm just happy to be here with you."

My heart fluttered and my face started to blush.

"Oh Deacon, that's so sweet. I love you."

Deacon froze in time. It took me a second to realize what I'd said.

"You love me?" He asked, quietly.

"Oh my gosh. It just slipped out. I'm sorry."

He laughed. “Why would you be sorry? That’s the best thing I’ve heard in forever. I love you too, Tilda Loxley.”

Deacon pulled me close and kissed me.

It was official. We both loved each other passionately.

“So, what does that mean? We’re still in a crappy situation. In two days, we must go our separate ways, again. I hate that. I hate the idea of having to say goodbye indefinitely to you.”

“Then don’t. Come to Ireland and stay with me.”

I laughed at his insane idea that was obviously a joke.

“I’m not kidding.”

“My kids are back home. I can’t leave them.”

“Bring them with you. Bring George. Bring your life and be with me. I have a house and if it isn’t big enough, we’ll get a bigger house. We can put the kids in school, you could do whatever it is you want to do. Finish your Bucket List in Ireland, with me.”

For a brief moment, I imagined just picking up our lives to start a new one with Deacon.

“It’s not realistic. I can’t do that to the kids. They need a say. Plus, their grandparents are the only link they have to their father. I can’t deny them that. It’s not fair to either parties.”

“Well I can’t pick up and leave my life either. My dad made it clear that he wants to retire soon. The long nights are killing him, and my sister can’t take over the business. She’s got four kids and a husband who spends enough time at the pub as it is. I'm the only one left."

"When were you going to tell me that you had no intention of coming back to me? You promised me, Deacon. You promised you would come back to me."

"I'm here aren't I?"

"Yes, and in a couple days we say goodbye. Again."

I felt so stupid. Here, I had let myself fall in love with this young man who hadn't a clue what it was like to be a grown up. I had kids. I had a life. He had a pub.

Needless to say, the rest of our days in Venice were not perfect. I almost wished we'd had this miserable conversation the last day instead of the first day. Kissing in the gondola under the Bridge of Sighs was not going to be as romantic as I thought. I hoped Aunt Beebie wouldn't be too disappointed.

Deacon sat on the sofa, trying to find something on Netflix to distract from our awkward conversation. It didn't seem to be helping him.

"Okay, I know you're upset, but I'm hungry and I think you are too. Let's go find something to eat. I insist you be my date tonight, Tilda Loxley." Deacon said in a tone deeper than his normal register.

I laughed at his assertiveness. "I suppose you're right, Deacon Kelly. I do have to eat."

We walked downstairs to a popular restaurant, also recommended by our host.

The waiter sat us at the last available table outside and handed us our menus. It was all in Italian, but thanks to my basic Italian language online courses, (and google translate) I was able to help us manage the foreign words.

I opted for a seafood tagliatelle, while Deacon found a wild boar ragú with pappardelle that met his liking.

We didn't go into any further discussion about our relationship, choosing to simply enjoy the food, wine and Venetian atmosphere.

Once we finished our dinner, we walked back to our apartment and conquered the miles of stairs up to the apartment door. Deacon and I spent the rest of the night snuggling on the sofa watching mindless television.

The following morning, we walked to the Piazza San Marco to tour the Doge's Palace. I found the entire city magnificent, although Sam was correct. The city is so packed full of tourists, it is difficult to take it all in peacefully. I decided to follow Sam's recommendation to visit the nearby islands for a break.

We took a water bus to Torcello Island. Deacon and I relaxed by the water, enjoying a glass of wine and snack. It was nice to see the chaos of the main island from a distance. The only noise on Torcello was a local seagull demanding food and perhaps the engine of a water taxi docking their boat.

We spent our day pretending everything was just fine in our relationship. That Deacon didn't have to go home to Ireland, instead of accompanying me to the U.S.

I woke up on our last day in Venice feeling sad and defeated. Even the magic elixir of Italian coffee in Venice couldn't make me feel better. I wanted to forget everything and just enjoy my time with Deacon. I just didn't quite know how to do that.

"Are you ready to do the gondola ride?" Deacon asked, remembering my main reason for coming on this trip.

"Yes, let's go ahead and get it over with."

"Get it over with? Tilda, I'm sorry. I didn't mean to ruin your experience here. We'll figure something out. I love you. People in love fight sometimes. It doesn't mean the end."

But it felt like the end to me. My heart had closed. I still loved him, which was the exact reason for that closure. I couldn't allow myself to get hurt again, although I knew it was too late for that.

It was a quiet walk from our apartment to the main tourist areas. As we approached the canal, it was easy to find a gondolier ready to help me check off one more thing off my aunt's bucket list. I handed the man, dressed in the required blue and white striped shirt, the 80 euros while Deacon helped me enter the gondola.

We sat quietly and closely, holding hands and not speaking about our differences or future.

It might have been the saddest gondola ride our

gondolier Nicola had ever experienced.

He cleared his throat and said with his thick Italian accent, “It is customary for lovers to kiss under the Bridge of Sighs. It will give you eternal love.”

As we approached our bridge, Deacon and I looked at one another.

“I want eternal love more than anything, Tilda.” Deacon softly put his hand on my cheek and kissed me. I didn’t want the kiss to end. I didn’t want us to end. But I didn’t see how a tale about an ancient bridge would help.

We finished our gondola ride and packed our things for the water taxi to the airport. We said our goodbyes. His destination, Dublin while mine was much further away.

I was thankful for my sleeping aid for the long flight back.

Chapter 12

After a miserable experience in Venice, I was elated to be home with my kids and George. I was completely lost and heartbroken. Deacon tried multiple times to reach me, but I had rebuffed all attempts during the month I'd been home. I needed to distance myself a bit from him. Geographical distance wasn't enough. This lady needed a detox from all men and ideas of love.

What better way to do that than a girl's trip to a haunted plantation home?

Cassie, Tabitha and I flew to Baton Rouge and rented a car to drive to the small town of St. Francisville. Summer had already arrived in the South Louisiana town per my once glossy, straight hair.

I'd reserved the Caretaker's Quarters house. I thought if we did have any sort of paranormal experience, we'd be in one room. Maybe even one bed.

"So, Tilda what happened with your fella?" Tabitha asked as she unloaded her suitcase and pulled out her toiletries bag.

I lay my head down on the bed and simply said, "It just didn't work out."

"Tilda lost her mind at the idea of moving to Ireland to be with Deacon." Cassie added.

"Cassie! I didn't lose my mind. I can't just pick up everything and move my kids for some teenage romance."

"It's not a teenage romance, Tilda. Just because

he's younger than you, doesn't mean it isn't legitimate. I think you know that and that's why you are fighting it."

"So, I suppose you're Team Deacon right now." I blurted out, not really meaning any of it.

Tabitha, looking a bit shell shocked at the conversation asked, "Ok what is happening? I just wanted to know the story. I didn't mean to open up a hot mess. Let's change the subject."

"Tilda," Cassie said, "I'm not Team anybody. I just want you to let yourself be happy and live. Deacon loves you. So maybe you don't move to Ireland, but you can't just shut the door on him. Let him explain. Have a discussion at least!"

"It takes more than love, Cassie." I said quietly.

"Yes, I know."

Cassie sat on our bed and began to cry. When I say cry, I mean that moment when you watch a sad Hallmark movie that opens the floodgates to every piece of grief you've ever experienced.

Tabitha and I both looked at each other, not really knowing what to do. We rushed over to comfort her.

Even though Cassie blubbered, I was able to make out a few words. Her husband wanted a divorce.

Cassie sobbed between saying, "He said he isn't happy and thinks it would be best for our family. We spend so much time apart anyway."

"Oh Cassie, I'm so sorry." I felt awful for her. Cassie's husband made very good money and they seemed happy when they were together, but to be honest, I didn't know him all that well. He was gone almost all the time for work and Cassie never gave the impression it bothered her.

"Was he being unfaithful?" Tabitha asked, rubbing Cassie's back.

"No. No, he said he wasn't. I guess I believe him. He wants me to keep the house, so the kids' lives aren't disturbed too much. They'll see him on weekends, just not at home now." She squealed in anguish.

"Well I think it's time to pop this sucker open now." Tabitha pulled out her bottle of champagne. She pulled off the towels and ice packs that were strategically placed in order to keep it chilled.

Well done Tabitha. Well done.

"I think there are some glasses in the bathroom. I'll go get some." Tabitha came back with three highball glasses.

So, they weren't long stem flutes. We were in survival mode here. I would've pulled out a red Solo cup if necessary.

We poured a glass for each of us and we sipped our champagne.

"Oh wait! There's one more glass in there." Tabitha came out with a fourth glass and poured a smidge into it.

"Who's that for?" Cassie asked, confused, wiping away her tears.

"For the ghost. If I was haunting this place, I'd want a glass of booze as well. It's my peace offering in case somebody wants to harass me tonight." Tabitha replied to the air, as though the ghost might be there listening to our nonsense.

Tabitha's ghostly idea completely took Cassie out of her funk. "Oh my god Tabitha. That's hilarious. I think you'll fit in well with us," she said as she took a sip of her drink.

Tabitha is crazy, I thought. However, as I thought about it, I didn't think her idea was that farfetched after all. We might not have a single ghost encounter tonight but it's never a bad idea to think ahead and keep all of our spirits happy. Especially the dead ones.

We drank our champagne, left the glass for our spirit friend and headed over to the main house for afternoon tea.

The home was absolutely charming. Exactly what you would imagine a Southern Plantation home to be. It was the epitome of Southern charm. Pretty and elegant polished antiques, sparkling chandeliers, delicate bone china and of course, polite and welcoming Southern ladies.

"Welcome to The Grande Oaks. Are you here for afternoon tea?" A lady, possibly in her sixties directed us to the Tea Room. We had several tables to choose from. Each table had a 3-tiered serving tray filled with finger sandwiches, delicate cookies, scones and pastries.

Once seated, another lady, Greta, took our tea order and brought out cream and sugar. It was an excellent distraction from our current life problems. The three of us sat there in awe. Like little girls at their first fancy dress party. All we needed were matching American Girl dolls.

“So, ladies where are y’all staying?” Greta asked, pouring our tea into our intricately decorated china cups.

“We are in the Caretaker’s Cottage. It’s stunning by the way.”

“Oh, that’s one of our most active accommodations. Everyone who stays there usually has some type of experience.” Greta said, nonchalantly.

We all looked at each other and gulped. As much as we laughed and talked about a haunting, I don’t think any of us were prepared for it.

“Don’t worry ladies. Nobody has ever been harmed. The ghosts just like to let y’all know they’re around. If you’re respectful, you shouldn’t have any problems. We had some of those ghost hunting fellas come one time and got the spirits all riled up. They broke one of my antique lamps. Scoundrels.”

“The ghost hunters broke your lamp?” Cassie asked.

“No dear, the ghost. They were so upset at being provoked, they knocked over a lamp in protest. The ghost hunters were the scoundrels though. Definitely. Anyway, you ladies enjoy your afternoon tea.”

Greta moved on to the other tables of guests, leaving us with a lot to think about.

Tabitha finally spoke and said, “See who’s the

crazy one now? They might like my gesture of including a glass of bubbly for them."

I still cringed at the thought of wasting any champagne, although maybe she was right.

After our tea, we took a little walking tour of the grounds. There was a lot of history on this land. A lot of it was related to the slaves forced to work on the plantation. An awful part of our American history that should never be forgotten.

"I think I need a rest before dinner. Shall we go back to our cottage?" Cassie had worked extremely hard to enjoy herself, or at least give the impression.

Tabitha groaned and pulled her shoes off for the last 100 feet of walking, "My feet hurt. I don't think I should have worn these sandals. They say a wedge is more comfortable, but I question that theory. My feet feel like bricks right now."

"That's because your wedges are five inches high, Tabitha. Feet shouldn't be in the air that long," I said, I stopped wearing high heels after my kids were born. It was quite sad, but my feet just couldn't tolerate them anymore.

We walked into our cottage to see everything looking just as we left it. The ghosts decided to not remake our beds after we'd sat on them earlier.

"Hey! Did one of you drink the ghost's champagne?" Tabitha called out from the far side of the room.

"Nope." Cassie and I said in unison.

"Well it's gone! Somebody must have drunk it.

Did housekeeping think it was a tip?"

"Housekeeping would not have been here. We just checked in."

We all looked at each other. We were realizing the same thing.

"Do you have any more champagne or wine, Tabitha? I think I'm ready for another drink." Cassie said, changing into her lounge clothes.

Tabitha pulled out a new bottle of wine and held it in the air, "As a matter of fact, I do. I picked up a bottle of Merlot when we got gas near the airport. I had a feeling we might need it."

Tabitha poured a glass for each of us, including the ghost and said excitedly, "Let's play two truths and a lie!"

"Huh? Is that like truth or dare?" I asked, never hearing of the game.

"One of us says two truthful things and then one that's not true. The others guess which one is a lie! It's fun. Plus, it's a good way to get to know each other. Okay, I'll go first!"

Tabitha took a chug of wine.

"Okay. One, I am a true blonde. Two, I look up old boyfriends on Facebook. Three, I once tried out for American Idol and got through the first round.

Cassie and I both looked at each other. I had no idea what was the truth or a lie. I guess I did need to learn more about our new friend.

"I have the answer." Cassie announced after finishing her wine. You, Tabitha Wells are NOT a true blonde!"

"Nope." Tabitha responded calmly.

"Well, I have a 50/50 chance now. It is a lie that you look up old boyfriends on Facebook!"

Tabitha laughed, "Are you serious? You guys have never looked up old boyfriends to see if they're bald and fat now? We need to add that to our list of things to do tonight."

"Okay. So, you didn't audition for American Idol. I don't know why I didn't say that was the lie. That's crazy." Cassie said, pouring yet another glass of wine and taking a huge sip before she ran to the bathroom.

"Actually, I did try out, but I didn't make it. I'm a terrible singer. I don't know what I was thinking. Monica..." Tabitha abruptly stopped.

"It's okay, you can talk about her. If we're going to be friends, you can't eliminate her from everything we talk about." I said, softly. It was true. I had to allow Tabitha to deal with her grief, despite the circumstances.

"Monica used to tell me I could do anything. Even though she was the younger one, I felt like she was older and wiser than I ever would be." I could see her start to tear up when Cassie returned from the bathroom.

"Tilda, it's your turn! I'm sure there are some things we don't know about you." Cassie exclaimed. "Wait! I know! I'll do it! Tabitha you guess."

Drunk Cassie was always much louder than sober Cassie.

"All right! One, Tabitha once wore contact lenses to change her eyes from brown to blue. Two, she never got rid of her husband's clothes and still has them in her closet. Three, she once wrote a letter to all five of the New Kids on the Block and invited them to her birthday party at the roller rink.

"Cassie! Those are all true! Oops. Sorry Tabitha."

Tabitha laughed, "That's so funny! But wait, you still have the clothes of your late husband, who cheated on you, taking up valuable closet space?"

I quietly replied behind my glass of wine, "Yes."

"I think I speak for Cassie as well in saying, it's time to get rid of that shit."

Cassie exclaimed, "Yes! Get rid of that shit!"

"I know. I'll do it when we get back. I know it's time."

Cassie looked over at the fourth wine glass and said, "You guys! Where's the wine we left for the ghost?!"

Tabitha looked over and said, "What do you mean? It's right…it was right…it's gone!"

Seeing how drunk Cassie was already, I said, "Cass, did you drink it by mistake?"

"No! I've been sitting on the bed the whole time! I just got up to go to the bathroom a minute ago."

That night, I was glad Tabitha got the bed to herself and I had to share with Cassie. I was grateful to someone to grab ahold of if a ghost pinched my toes. I was mostly glad because I could talk to Cassie more about her divorce announcement.

"Cassie, are you going to be okay? I mean with

the divorce?"

"Yes, I think I will. I'll have to go back to work, but that's not a terrible thing." Cassie had been a CPA at an investment firm in her previous life, before having twins. I didn't know her then. I've heard stories of how she worked in a big high rise and practically ran the department she worked in. I was fortunate she was able to refer me to an excellent financial advisor from her former life.

"But will you be okay emotionally, I mean. Losing a husband, regardless of the circumstances is difficult. Trust me, I know." I whispered.

"I will with time. Tilda, we've been headed this direction for a long time. I was just in denial. Weekend husband, no time for fighting or anything else for that matter. It was a recipe for disaster. I'm just glad we've been able to talk and not hate each other. I don't want that for Jameson and Michael. My mom and dad's divorce was awful. They still can't be around each other. When I had the twins, they got into a fight in the waiting area. Two grown ass people, shouting at each other in the maternity ward."

"I'm sorry Cassie. I'm sorry you're going through all this."

Cassie rolled over to her side and whispered, "Me too, Tilda. Me too. Goodnight."

"Goodnight."

We all slept soundly that night without having a single toe disturbed.

In the morning, we awoke to sunshine and birds

chirping in the nearby Oak trees. The air was already feeling humid after an early rain. I was ready to pack up and go into the town to see more of St. Francisville. Our flight out of Baton Rouge didn't leave until early evening giving us plenty of time to explore.

At checkout, we asked if it was customary for housekeeping services to come into our lodging midday.

"Oh no. Not unless you requested something. No, we like to give our patrons their privacy. Why do you ask?"

"Well, we left a glass of champagne on the table. When we came back from our tea and tour, it was empty." We didn't really have an answer for the glass of Merlot that disappeared either, but we chose not to share that story.

"Hmm. Well I can tell you at that time of day, we only have one housekeeper still on site. She was with me, folding towels and organizing toiletries for the next day. Nobody was in your room helping themselves to champagne." The lady laughed and added, "Well, no living person. It was probably our young, ghost Yvette being sneaky."

Not wanting to get our resident ghost in trouble I said, "Well, to be clear, we did leave it for a ghost. We just didn't think anyone would actually take it."

"Oh, that's sweet of you. That's probably why you didn't get hassled. Yvette is one of our previous, err, residents. She was a young slave girl who died of typhoid fever. Terrible thing. Her resting place is behind the cottage y'all stayed in. I bet she appreciated you thinking of her."

Cassie, Tabitha and I all gulped, walking out the door.

We rolled our bags out to the car, but I felt like I had one more thing to do.

"Hold on guys. I forgot something. I'll meet you in a sec."

I ran back to our cottage, which wasn't far from the parking area. Sure enough, behind it, was a gravestone marked for Yvette.

"Goodbye, sweet girl. I hope you enjoyed your champagne." Just as I said my goodbyes, a little bird appeared in the tree behind us. It chirped at me with a beautiful little song. It was probably just one of the many birds that surrounded the grounds, but I imagined it to be Yvette. A peaceful, sweet little bird with the freedom to sing and fly wherever she pleased.

Chapter 13

It was early July and a few weeks since I'd heard anything out of Deacon. After a solid month of trying to communicate with me, I figured he gave up on me. I hated the way we left things in Venice. I hated not talking to him. Mostly, I hated myself for leading him to believe I had given up.

Cassie's unfortunate marriage situation brought me some new perspective. I still didn't feel ready to move to Ireland. But she was right. I did need to at least talk to him. Here I had this wonderful man who wanted me in his life so much he invited me to live in his home country. He deserved to hear back from me, so I sent a text asking him to call me, hoping it wasn't too late.

I wondered what Aunt Beebie would have advised me to do with my Deacon dilemma. Her Bucket List didn't have any indicators. It did have some items I still needed to tackle though.

I was still avoiding the two most terrifying tasks, the hot air balloon and posing nude for an art class. Honestly, I don't know what that lady was thinking. How can posing nude for an art class be part of anybody's Bucket List?!

In typical avoidance, I chose to focus on the other pending item. Teach a class.

Our community center has excellent resources for every walk of life. They recently lost one of their volunteers who taught Intro to English classes for Non-English speakers on Wednesday nights. Apparently, the young lady, a college student, quit because she was taking a job overseas.

Mind you, I've never taught a class. However, I do know English since it's my first and only language. I wish I could count Italian as my second language, but I'm still getting there. I can order gelato now. That must count for something.

I was a bit nervous as the students casually entered the room. Nevertheless, I did not want to show it. I mean, it wasn't like I was teaching some high-risk teenagers. They were adults who truly wanted to be there.

"Okay class. My name is Tilda Loxley and I'm going to teach you to speak English!" I said, feeling excited and proud. The class however just stared at me. "Oh right, sorry. You don't speak English, so you have no idea what I'm saying. Hm." Don't panic, Tilda.

"Let's start with introductions. Hello, I am Tilda." I motioned for the class to repeat. They caught on quickly, repeating the *Hello, I am Tilda*.

I pointed to the man in the front row and asked him his name. "Hello, what is your name?" He just looked at me and said, "Hello, I am Tilda."

"Oh, no I meant, your name. What is *your* name?" The man looked over at the younger lady sitting next to him.

"Fuck, Omar! Your name. Omar!"

I was a bit taken aback by her foul language but impressed by her English. She seemed to know more than some of the others. I'd have to rely on her a bit.

"It's okay, Omar. We'll keep working on it." I moved on to the next person. "Hello, I am Tilda. What's your name?"

The pretty lady looked at me proudly and said "Hello. I am Shira. Now fuck off."

I didn't know how to respond. Why did this lady swear so much? Had I done something to offend her?

I continued with the lesson, doing an introduction with each student. Since we only had seven people in the class, it went by rather quickly, all things considered. Thankfully, none of the others told me to fuck off.

The class was a mixture of ages and ethnicities. There was a woman from China, four men from Central America, Omar from Turkey and Shira from Israel.

We went over basics, like the alphabet and numbers on the first day. I hadn't taken a foreign language class since college, but I think that's what we did in the beginning. That was a million years ago though, so who knows really.

When class ended, I caught up with Shira, who seemed to have the best grip on English.

"Shira, wait."

She looked back in fear, which surprised me.

"Oh no. Fuck."

"What? No, it's okay. Question?"

"No. No question. Bye."

"No, Shira, wait! I have a question!"

"Oh, sorry. Fuck."

"Are you okay, Shira? You seem scared. Is someone making you be here without your consent?" I had read stories about young women who are enticed by men to come to the United States with lies of a better life. They turn out to be criminals and force the women into sex trafficking. Shira, however just looked at me with a quizzical stare.

"Am I in trouble? I can speak English. Kind of. Better than fucking Omar, that's for sure."

"What? No. If you can speak English, why are you in this class?"

"I wanted practice. I'm starting my graduate classes in the fall. I don't want to sound stupid."

"Well, first off, you don't sound stupid. You do sound like a sailor who just stepped off the ship for the first time in six months. Why all of the F bombs?"

"In the movies, everybody swears like that. I learned how to speak English by watching Quentin Tarantino movies."

Good lord. It's a wonder she even came to America with that as her source of cultural information. Those movies are probably more violent than any Israeli city she's from.

"Ah, I see. Well, a bit of advice. Maybe stop with the swearing. People don't do that here in general conversation with the strangers." I also felt the need to add, "Oh, and people don't shoot, stab or roundhouse kick as casually as they do in Tarantino movies."

"What do you think I'm a savage? I don't stab anyone unless they deserve it." Shira said, walking to her luxury SUV. I stood there for a minute hoping I wouldn't be one of those people.

I got to my car and hurriedly checked my phone. I had it turned off while I taught the class. The cellular reception in the old brick building was awful I didn't want to drain my already ancient battery. Yes, I've inherited $2.8 million but I just haven't gotten around to a new phone. I had other priorities, although I was excited to get the newest and fanciest phone for once.

Deacon hadn't responded to my text. I guess I didn't blame him. My heart broke all over again.

I let out my own F bombs driving home. I felt incredibly stupid for thinking everything would turn out fine.

I made it home before the kids went to sleep. I hired the same babysitter from the first night I met Deacon. What she must have thought about me? Oh, that night was terribly embarrassing. Still, the kids liked her, and she seemed responsible for $10 an hour.

I walked into Logan's room to see both kids in his bed, watching a YouTuber play Roblox.

"Did you two have a good night with Maddie?" Pause. No response. "Hellooooo. Did you have a good night?" No response. I finally yelled to my comatose zombie children. "Hey!!!!"

"Mommy! You're home!" Livia exclaimed, snapping out of her hypnotic state and running over to hug me.

"Yes! So? Did you have a good night with Maddie?"

Livia walked back over to Logan's bed. "Yes. We watched some SpongeBob and that Henry Danger episode I like. Then Maddie played Hide and Seek with us! It was fun."

"How about you, Logan? Everything went okay?"

"Yeah, it was fine." Logan was at the age where he resented having a babysitter, but also knew he was far too young to be left alone to take care of himself or his little sister. So, he just groaned and grunted about it all. Welcome to the 'Tweens.'

"Liv, are you sleeping in Logan's room tonight?" Sometimes, Logan would let her have a slumber party in his room. They would watch movies on the iPad until they fell asleep. Since it was summer, I didn't have an issue with it. In fact, I thought it was rather sweet.

"Yes."

"It's okay Logan? For Livia to stay in here tonight?"

"Yes."

"Did you guys brush your teeth?"

"Yes."

"Okay then, I'll say goodnight. I love you guys. Sleep tight."

"Don't let the bedbugs bite!" They said in unison. We had a routine that never seemed to get old and I loved it. I dreaded the day they both learned bedbugs were indeed real and a current hotel epidemic.

I got ready for bed. Then checked my phone for the perhaps one-hundredth time since I'd gotten out of class. Still no Deacon.

I went to bed with some old Parks & Rec episodes playing in the background and tried to sleep my sadness away.

Chapter 14

I was absolutely disgusted with my feelings last night, I shut my phone completely off and didn't turn it on when I first woke up. Yawning, I walked to the kitchen to make a coffee. The kids and George were still sleeping, which allowed me to sit in the quiet July morning with my cup of coffee. If I were completely irresponsible, I would splash a shot of Bailey's in it, but I wasn't. Plus, I needed to refrain from all things Irish. Instead, I decided to invite my new Israeli, Turkish, Central American and Chinese students to an Independence Day barbeque at my house.

I also sent Cassie a text to let her know I was up and ready for coffee company. Sometimes Cassie will come over in the early hours of the morning and have coffee with me. Her husband was at home with the kids today. I think coming over for coffee gave Cassie a break from her awkward home life.

Cassie walked through the door, carrying her flavored creamer and a package of coffee pods. I made her a coffee and let her know about my larger guest list.

Cassie took a bite of the muffin I handed her and said, "You don't even know these people." Just because they want to learn English doesn't mean they aren't serial killers or something."

"Cassie, you're starting to sound like me now.

Not every stranger is a serial killer. A wise woman once told me that."

"This wise woman wants you to know my cousin is trying to reach you."

My heart stopped.

"Cousin?"

"Yes, my cousin. Deacon? The handsome Irishman who fell in love with you and then pissed off back to his luscious land? That cousin. Apparently, he dropped his phone in a pint at work when he saw you texted him."

"He dropped his phone when I texted him. That is so sweet!"

"Anyway, Tilda. He gave me a new number. It's his home phone. He's waiting for his new phone to come in. It seems he's quite desperate to talk to you."

I tried to act natural and calm.

Deacon wasn't blowing me off. He dropped his phone in a pint of beer!!!

I took the number from Cassie's hand, moved to a quiet room for privacy and after a few failed attempts at calling an out of country number, I heard a ring. The phone rang. And rang. And rang.

"Hello?" Finally, someone answered. Unfortunately, it wasn't the person I had hoped it would be. Instead, it was the voice of a lady. Super awkward.

"Oh, um, hello. I'm calling for Deacon?" In the age of cell phones and texting, I don't think I have called a boy like this since high school.

"Is this Tilda? From America?" The lady sounded delighted, and roughly my age. Please don't be his mother. Please don't be his mother.

"This is Deacon's mother, Mary! I'm so happy you have called. He's been rather distraught, our Deacon." Yikes. I hope she didn't blame me.

"I'm sorry for any err, distraughtness I've caused. Is he there, by chance?" I had forgotten my main reason for calling in the first place, to speak with Deacon.

"Oh no love. He's out. He had some errands to run before his shift at the pub starts. If I don't see him before he goes to work, I can leave a message for him there. Is there anything you want me to say? Oh Tilda, I think he's rather keen on you, if you don't mind me saying so. He's barely eaten since he's been back."

"Really? He hasn't been eating. Has he been out, um, socializing?" Shame on you, Tilda. I thought to myself. The guy has been starving himself due to depression and all you can think about is whether or not he's hooking up with some pretty Irish hussies.

"Well he has his friends from school he sees. He's been working a lot though, what with his father in such a poor state. It's not looking good I'm afraid. The doctor doesn't give him a lot of time."

What? Deacon never mentioned anything about his father. Was that why he rushed back home?

"Oh, um, yes I'm so sorry. I won't keep you. Could you please let him know I called?"

"Of course, love. You take care of yourself and those precious children Deacon has told me about."

"Thank you, Mary. Bye-bye."

I came back to the living room. The kids were up, eating the cereal Cassie had fixed for them.

"Good morning sunshines!" I said overly cheery.

"Good morning." Logan and Livia said, completely focused on their Lucky Charms and cartoons.

"Cassie, do you need more coffee?" I motioned her to the kitchen.

"Oh sure!" She caught on quickly and followed me to the Nespresso machine.

"I've just had the strangest conversation. It seems Deacon hasn't been forthright with us. Did you know your uncle is in failing health?"

"No, nobody has told me anything. Typical. I'm always the last to know when it comes to all of the family over there. What did Mary say?"

"She said Deacon's been running everything, hanging out with friends from school, when he has time and not seeing any hussies.

"Mary said he wasn't hanging out with hussies? That doesn't seem like her."

"No, I just gathered that portion of the conversation based on my inquisitive questions. I thought you might be interested, that's all. He must have rushed home because of his father's poor health. Do you think?"

"Maybe? I guess he didn't want to worry anybody. So, you didn't get to speak to him?"

"No. And now I have to set my focus on a 4th of July barbeque when all I want to do is hop on a plane to Dublin and find Deacon."

"Well, obviously, you are not obliged to hold this party if you don't feel like it. Especially since you invited a bunch of strangers who don't speak English. Not that there's anything wrong with that. It just makes conversation a bit awkward."

"So far it's just one person and she actually speaks pretty good English, despite her overuse of the F word."

"This is going to be an interesting party. I'll be back with the kids around 1:30? Is that good? I'll help you set up. Hopefully you'll have more information regarding my mysterious cousin by then."

While the kids hung out, I got to working on food preparation. I started marinating chicken, cutting up veggies, making the macaroni salad and coleslaw. I stacked my burgers in parchment paper, pulled out the buns from the pantry for later and put beer and soda in the cooler. I basically prepped my 4th of July spread like a chef in a busy five-star restaurant.

I did everything I possibly could to distract myself from waiting to hear back from Deacon. The kids and I cleaned up the backyard and got tables ready to put the food and drinks out. Finally, after about five hours of waiting, my phone rang.

I almost felt like couldn't breathe. What was he going to say? Was he going to tell me to fuck off? Was he going to tell me the truth about everything?

"Hello?" I answered the phone, knowing it would be him but still terrified.

"Tilda?" Deacon took a deep breath

"Deacon?"

"God, Tilda. It's so good to hear your voice." He sounded tired, hoarse and relieved. "I've wanted to talk to you for so long. Why did you ignore me? I sent about a hundred messages."

"I'm sorry, Deacon. I was hurting and the way I dealt with it was to close myself off. I'm sorry. I should have been an adult and told you how I felt. I haven't done this for a while."

"I'm sorry as well. I should've told you everything that was happening. My dad is sick, Tilda. Really sick. He didn't tell any of us, so when I left for America, I didn't know."

He choked up. I think it was the first time I heard him be so vulnerable. I had no idea what to do or say.

"What can I do to help?" I asked trying not to cry myself. I didn't know his dad, but the situation sounded so hopeless. I knew what it felt like to lose a parent. I'd lost both of mine. I'd also lost Aunt Beebie.

"Well, you could pick up your phone and reply to

my texts. That helps."

"I'm sorry."

"I'm joking. I mean, I'm not, but I'm not trying to make you feel bad. I wish you were here. Or I was there. Fuck. But then I wouldn't be here. I don't what to do. Anyway, how are you?"

"I'm fine. I guess. I started teaching a class for Non-English speakers. I have no idea what I'm doing but I think I'm helping. I've only done one class so far. I'm having some people over today for a barbeque. It's our Independence Day today. I invited my class last night."

It felt silly talking about my mundane goings on when there were far more important things to discuss. I just didn't want to bring it up and I don't think Deacon did either.

"I miss you, Tilda. There are some days when I think about you and I feel like I can't breathe."

From the other room I could hear Cassie shouting that she was here. I could hear other voices in the background as well.

"Oh shit. Am I too early?" I knew that profanity anywhere and I'd only known it for about 24 hours.

"Shit." I said out loud to Deacon.

"What? What's happening?"

"I invited the students from last night's class to my 4th of July party. The only one who could come is Shira from Israel. She swears like a truck driver. I'm sorry Deacon. I guess I should let you go. For the night. Let you go for the night. We'll talk about the other stuff later?"

He let out a breath and said, "That sounds like a great idea. I love you, Tilda." And then he hung up. He didn't even give me the chance to tell him I loved him too.

"Tilda! Where are you? Oh, are you okay? Is it Deacon?" Thankfully it was Cassie who found me.

"Yes. I mean no. Deacon and I finally talked. Things are better. I just wish we could figure out what to do."

"Well right now you have a backyard with some hungry people waiting on an American 4th of July party. It seems Shira brought friends and food."

I walked out and saw new kids running around. I assumed they were Shira's.

"Hi Tilda! This is my husband, Erez and my kids are running somewhere." She handed me a huge bowl of salad and pointed over to her kids who were running around with Logan, Liv and Cassie's twins.

"I didn't hear you say you were serving salad, so I brought some. I always eat salad. Most American food has too many calories for me." I was confused by her comment. The woman was skinny as a stick. Since the salad looked wonderful, I saw no need to fuss.

I handed a beer to Erez, who thanked me. He looked less than thrilled to be the only man at the party. I felt bad. In a perfect situation, Cassie's husband would be here. I would have Deacon and the men could go off on their own to talk about guy stuff.

"Is this a typical Independence Day?" Shira asked, sipping her wine spritzer.

"Pretty much. We just hang out and eat. Then when it gets dark, we set off fireworks. We should've had the party at Cassie's house. She has a pool. I just have sprinklers, I'm afraid."

"Why are you afraid? Are you afraid of the water?" Shira asked.

"No, no. It's just something we say. It's more like an apology for my not very exciting backyard."

"Are fucking kidding me?" She pointed to the swings and said, "You have all of this equipment for kids to play. If they get too hot, they come and have a cold drink. Look, they're having a good time. Don't say sorry."

They were having a good time. Shira's two daughters were chasing Logan while the other kids chased in opposite directions.

"Shira! You're still f-bombing. But you're right. I need to stop apologizing." That reminded me of a book I wanted to download that spoke to that very thing.

"Shit, I'm sorry. I'm working really hard to not swear as much. The moms at my daughter's pre-school stopped wanting to have coffee with me. I think it's my swearing. Or they don't like Israeli people. Maybe both." Shira explained nervously while tossing her kale salad and putting a portion on Cassie's plate.

Cassie put her plate up to the large salad bowl and said, "Don't worry about those moms. Tell them to fuck off. You make a great kale salad by the way."

I felt the need to clarify Cassie's *fuck off* comment to our new friend. "Yes, you do. But to be clear, do not tell them to fuck off. Cassie just means to ignore their behavior."

"Oh right," Cassie said. "Yes, don't literally tell them that. But what I mean is we have a lot of judgmental people in this town. A lot of bitches."

"In Israel we don't talk about you behind your back. We tell you to your face if we don't like you. I like you ladies. You're good bitches."

Cassie and I nearly spit out our salad with laughter. It felt good to laugh.

"Cheers to that." I said as Cassie and I tapped our wine glasses together.

Chapter 15

July was halfway over which meant the kids would be starting school in a month or so. The school year seemed to start earlier and earlier every year. While Logan and Livia were a lot of work, because they were kids, I enjoyed having the freedom with them. No strict bedtimes. They could eat breakfast when they felt like it, instead of having to shove a cereal bar down their throats when they got out of the car at the school drop off. I didn't have to fight about homework and reading assignments. We could just enjoy being together.

Still, I was restless. Mostly because I missed Deacon terribly. I felt helpless by the fact we were so far apart.

"Do you guys remember when we had those passports made last spring?" I had decided it was a good idea to get the kids passports when I was trying to decide where to go on our Northern Lights adventure, Alaska or Iceland.

"Huh? A passfort? What's that?" Livia asked.

"A passport!" Logan corrected.

"A passport is for travel outside of the United States. I'm thinking we need one more adventure before school starts next month. What do you say, guys? Feel like an adventure?"

They both jumped up and shouted excitedly, "Yay!"

Actually, they didn't. In fact, their response was

rather disappointing.

"Sure." Logan and Livia said returning to their previously scheduled zoning out.

"Well I'll take that as a yes. I'll start planning our trip!"

I knew exactly where I wanted to go…

I didn't have time to plan for George to tag along and since she *technically* is not an emotional support animal she would have to go in cargo on the airplane. I decided everyone would be much happier if she stayed back with Cassie and her family as the flight to Dublin is about 13 hours. I should have sprung for first class given my bank account. However, I refused to give my children that taste of luxury. So, I compromised on economy plus.

By the next day, plane tickets were purchased, and rental house was reserved. George was off to Cassie's and we were off to the airport.

"Mommy, I want to play Roblox." Livia said, settling down in her seat.

"Livia, I told you, we can't play Roblox on the airplane. You'll have to find a game that doesn't require internet."

Livia put down her iPad and proceeded to cry at the mere notion she would have to refrain from playing her favorite game.

"Mom, did you download the Captain America movie?"

"No, I thought I said you needed to do that?" Truthfully, I didn't remember any conversation about Captain America, but imagined I would have said something of the sort.

"Mom, you said you'd download my movies for me. I said I wanted to watch Captain America and Spiderman and you said *Okay, I'll get them downloaded. Now go take your shower* and then I went to take a shower."

How does a child remember something so vividly and yet can't remember when *I* ask him something important?

Now, there was no way of getting out of this because first of all, I didn't recall this conversation that my son has recited verbatim. Secondly, I did not download those movies because I didn't recall the conversation.

"Logan, I'm going to be honest here. I didn't download the movies. I downloaded a bunch of SpongeBob episodes, and a few other movies but not the ones you have spoken of. I'm sorry."

Logan looked at me with panic and disgust. In his eyes, I had completely let him down. I seriously hoped the next 13 hours would not consist of his evil eye and pouting.

"Logan, it's okay that mommy didn't do that. I have Spiderman on my iPad. You can watch it if you want." Livia said, taking off her headphones and offering her iPad to her big brother.

Logan relaxed, thanked Livia for her offer and traded his iPad with her.

"Phew. Thanks Liv." I whispered to my SpongeBob loving daughter and gave Logan a smile to help ease the tension. He smiled back. All was well.

Many, many hours later, we arrived at the busy Dublin Airport. Once we got through customs and retrieved our bags, we found the driver I arranged to pick us up.

I was surprising Deacon, so I rented an adorable Airbnb house in his town to fit the kids and me. I didn't want to burden his mother either. I was sure she had enough on her plate. I was also terrified to meet her. What if we were close in age? Or looked the same? Gross.

During the drive from the airport to the house, my nerves were calmed by the crisp Irish air. I was also calmed by the kids' excitement. This was their very first trip out of the country. Although to be honest, Alaska felt like a whole other continent.

We pulled up to the rental house and any nerves I had were calmed. The home was white brick with beautiful greenery around the front. I tapped in the electronic security code provided by the host and opened the door to our temporary home. The moment we entered, the kids ran upstairs to their room, which included a set of bunk beds. Livia was excited to share a room with her brother, while her brother was excited to claim the top bunk.

Although they were tired from the journey, the first thing they asked was for Deacon. After a quick shower to refresh, I sent him a text.

Hi! Thinking about you. What are you up to today?

Thinking about you as well. I have a day off so

relaxing. You?

We took a nice family trip to see a friend.

Sounds wonderful.

If you come to 5523 North Church St., you'll see for yourself.

??????

Do you know where that is?

Yes, I bloody know. It's around the corner from me. RU here??

Yes. I bloody am. Now get your ass over here.

Within about five minutes, Deacon's car raced into the driveway. I stood in the doorway, anxiously waiting for him. I was so excited I could've peed my pants. I wasn't going to tell him that, though.

He held me harder than I have ever felt him embrace me before. I practically held him up myself. We just held each other in the doorway for a couple of minutes.

"I can't believe you're actually here. God, I've missed you so much. Are the kids here as well?"

"Yes! I told you we came on a family trip. We missed you so here we are. The kids don't have school and I don't have to teach a class this week. We're here for eight days." When I said it out loud, it didn't seem very long.

"How long have you been here?" He loosened his hug and we walked into the house.

"Long enough for me to shower. The kids are hungry. Do you know where we can get something to eat?"

"As a matter of fact, I do. Come on."

We loaded into his car and went around the corner to a traditional looking pub called The Stag's Leap. A large statue of a deer greeted us outside the building as we entered it.

"Welcome to our pub. My dad is in the back. I'll introduce all of you."

We walked through the kitchen area to a small office space where his dad was busy jotting down some things.

Deacon took my hand and proudly said, "Dad, this is Tilda."

"Tilda, this is my dad, James."

James shook my hand warmly and said, "Tilda, I've heard nothing but wonderful things about you, since our Deacon has been back. He didn't tell us you were coming for a visit. And who is this?"

Deacon proudly said, "Dad, this is Logan and Livia. Tilda's pride and joy." Appearing somewhat shy, the two kids waved a hello to Deacon's father while standing close to me.

"Dad, I thought you were going home early today. Donno was supposed to come in to takeover, yeah?"

"Ah, he's late as usual. Your sister's choice in husbands has always astounded me. You'd think the second one would be better."

"I'll go around to see where he is. It's slow right now. We just have Patrick O'Toole at the bar to tend to. Do you feel up to making something for the kids and Tilda? They've not eaten since their plane landed. If not, I can start something quick."

"No, go find that useless lump. You kids fancy a burger and chips?"

Logan and Liv's eye widened, probably due to starvation by their mother. Note to self, always pack more snacks on long international journeys.

"I'll be back in a few. Doris is in the front handling the tap. I'll ask her to pour the kids a couple of sodas." He kissed me goodbye and headed out to find this useless Donno character.

While Deacon was out, the kids and I enjoyed our meal of burgers and fries, er, I mean chips. I helped clean up while James sat and talked to the Logan and Livia. He was easy to talk to, much like his son. I felt relieved to finally meet a member of his family and hoped the rest were as friendly and personable.

"Dor, can you get the kids another small coke, please?" James shouted from the kitchen. He looked over at me and said, "That's okay, mum?"

"Yes, it's fine." Spraying the dishes and adding them to the industrial dishwasher took me back to my restaurant days. It was a million years ago, but it all came back to me.

I found The Stag's Leap relaxing and comfortable, even as the patrons began to stroll in for the night and it got busy.

"What else can we do to help, James?" I asked, falling into the swing of things.

"You ever served drinks?"

"I used to wait tables if that's what you're asking."

"Well, things are starting to pick up. I think Dor could use some help if you're willing? Deacon should be back soon. Don't know what's taking him so long."

As James wondered about Deacon, his son walked in with a bloodied lip and nose.

"Deacon! What the hell happened?" James asked as he rushed to the door.

"I'm fine Dad. Donno and I just had a disagreement. I thought he was a lazy git and he disagreed." He said, smiling at me. How can someone with a bloodied-up face still be so incredibly hot?

"Come on then, let's go to the back and clean you up. Tilda, you got this?"

"Sure do! Kids, come have a seat over here while I help Ms. Doris."

Doris handed me a tray of pints and told me to bring it over to the table of fellas by the window. They had an ongoing tab, which continued to grow as the night went on.

Deacon cleaned up and came to help me. His dad went back to making chips and burgers in the kitchen.

"Deacon, I hate to leave you in this time of need, but the kids are absolutely exhausted. I think I need to get them home to bed."

His eyes twinkled as he said, "Home to bed. I love the way that sounds. My mum should be here in a bit. She's finishing her shift up at the hospital."

His mother was a nurse who worked twelve-hour days and then came straight to help out at the pub? I really needed to up my game and energy level.

We loaded into Deacon's car for the quick trip down the street and around the corner. Since it was getting dark, I appreciated the ride as evenings in Ireland were much cooler than back home and the kids and I hadn't dressed for chilly weather.

"Can I come back once I'm done tonight? Don't worry, I know you must be exhausted. I don't think I'll be able to sleep at home knowing I could be lying next to you."

"Of course. I'll leave a key for you under the mat. I might be out for the count though."

"Tilda, I can't thank you enough for your help tonight. You... being here is the answer to my prayers. I don't know how I'm going to say goodbye again."

"Let's not think about that. Now, you get back to that pub of yours. I'll be waiting for you." Granted, I would probably be snoring, but I would be waiting for him in spirit.

I have no idea what time Deacon came to bed but at some point, I felt his warm body next to mine. Keeping true to my word however, Deacon got nothing but loving snuggles. Jet lag had finally kicked my ass.

Jet lag had clearly kicked my children's asses also. Apart from Deacon, none of us woke up before 10:00 in the morning. The dark shades and cool Irish summer breeze complemented our need for sleep.

"Good morning, sunshine. Did you have a good sleep?" Deacon was sitting in the kitchen, drinking his coffee.

"Need coffee. STAT. But yes, I did have a good sleep. The best in a long time. How about you? That black eye is looking rough."

His poor face looked worse than it did last night. The blood was cleaned up although now he had horrible bruises around his nose and eyes.

"I have to sing tonight as well. Maybe I'll get more respect with my beat-up face."

I kissed his cheek and said, "That face should have all the respect, whether it's a pulpy mess or not. I can't wait to see this Donno. I hope he looks as bad."

"He does." Deacon smiled.

"Oh my gosh! You look terrible!" Logan said to Deacon as he walked into the kitchen. Livia, following behind, gasped when she saw Deacon's face. They must have been so tired last night, they didn't notice the bloody mess. This morning, however, they were bright eyed and a fully aware.

"What happened?!" Livia squealed.

"I got into a fight." Deacon lamented. "Not a way to solve your problems I'm afraid. But it felt good at the time!" He laughed and winked at the kids. Livia was not impressed.

"You shouldn't do that again." She said to Deacon. I smiled at Livia in agreement and handed her a chocolate milk.

"You my dear are a smart girl. I won't do that again." Livia, appearing satisfied with Deacon's response, turned her attention to her iPad in order to play an important game of Bubble Witch.

"What plans do you have today?" I asked, leaning against the counter and enjoying my second cup of coffee.

"Nothing for the day. Just work tonight. I'd love for you to be there."

"Me too, but I can't leave the kids."

"The kids can come, until 9:00 anyway. My cousin babysits. She's 16 and I reckon a lot more responsible than most of us in the family."

"Hmm. I'll talk to the kids about it. Will I get to meet your mother?"

"She's anxious to meet you so yes."

I was extremely nervous to meet her. I didn't know what expectations she had. Or if she had preconceived notions about an older lady stealing her only son. In my previous relationship, I never felt like I met the high standards of my mother-in-law. She put her son on a pedestal and refused to accept he could fall from it.

Would Deacon's mother be the same? Would she resent the twelve-year age difference? Or the instant family I was bringing into the relationship?

I started to panic at the mere thought of this relationship. What were we doing? It didn't seem like Deacon had any chance of leaving his life here. Did I even want him to? Was I going to pick up and uproot my family to join his? Did I even want to? Why had it gotten so hot in this room?

"Tilda, you're looking pale. Are you okay?" My rapid breathing and rising body temperature provided an unhealthy pallor. I needed to sit down. Quickly.

"I'm okay. I just got caught up in thoughts. I'll be fine."

I'll be fine. If I keep saying it must come to fruition. Right?

Chapter 16

I decided after my mild panic attack, a walk around the town would be nice. Deacon stayed back with the kids so they could watch cartoons and get dressed at their speed, which is typically not happening until at least three hours of intense sitting around doing nothing.

The morning still had an Irish summer chill to it, so I put on my light sweater and wore sneakers. I wished my summers back home were this pleasant. We don't live in an extremely walkable neighborhood either. My summer morning outings usually include an air-conditioned SUV and a few miles to the closest Dunkin Donuts.

I popped into a small coffee shop just down from our Airbnb home for more coffee that I didn't really need, but who cares? I'm on a vacation of sorts and this would be a nice way to meet the locals.

"Good morning. What can I get you?" The cheerful young lady behind the counter asked.

"Can I have a cappuccino and one of those scones, please?"

"Ooh are you American?" The dark haired, young lady asked as she pulled a scone from the display and placed it in the warmer.

"Yes. We're here visiting a friend."

"A friend from here?"

"Yes, Deacon Kelly. Do you know him?"

The young lady coughed. I noticed her posture tense up while she steamed my milk.

"Yes. I've known him my whole life. Did you meet him on his visit to America?"

I started to get a bit uncomfortable with the conversation. This girl had some history with my er...I didn't really know what he was to be honest. We hadn't had that conversation. Was he my boyfriend? Did we have titles? He did proclaim his love to me. That must be something. Right?

The girl just stared at me while watching my internal conversation, probably thinking I was a loon.

"Okay, well here's your cappuccino."

"I'm sorry, I was lost in a thought. Yes, his cousin is my best friend. My kids have taken quite a shine to him, so we came to visit on their summer break."

"Deacon and kids? Now I've heard it all. When he left us last year, he was on a mission to take over the world. I didn't think that would involve making friends with children. He never ceases to amaze me."

"Funny how that all works, isn't it?" I waved my hand with a hello gesture and said, "I'm Tilda, by the way."

"I'm Shar. Has Deacon ever mentioned me?" She asked, coyly.

This conversation was about to get incredibly awkward. What was I supposed to say?

No, he hasn't mentioned you, you silly girl! He's

sleeping with me and has declared his love!

Yes, I believe he has. What's that? Oh, I don't remember what he said because that's a lie and I have no idea who you are.

So, I just said, "I don't recall, to be honest."

Shar seemed somewhat disappointed yet satisfied with my response. She handed me my warm scone and returned to the kitchen. Probably to find a sharp knife and stab me in the eye. Or maybe to wash some dishes. Either way, I needed to finish my coffee quickly and get the fuck out of there.

And back to my place to ask Deacon who in the world Shar is.

"Oh god. You met Shar? She's been stalking me since nursery school."

"So, you weren't together?"

"Define 'together.'"

"Deacon, you know what I mean. Were you in a serious relationship before you took off for the States and found me?"

Deacon burst out laughing at my seemingly ridiculous scenario.

"Um, no. Have I kissed her on the playground? Yes. I also kissed Macey O'Neill, Carolyn Brennan, I may have kissed Connor O'Rourke on a dare one night, but I can assure you, it was only because you can't walk away from a dare. He's married to Macey O'Neill now and they have five kids, so don't worry about him. Or Shar Mahoney."

"This isn't funny. That girl looked like she wanted to kill me. In fact, I should probably puke up my scone because there might be cyanide in it."

"No need to puke anything. She might be in love with me, but the feelings have never been mutual. She's well aware of that. I did have a girlfriend about a year ago, but she's married now."

"You had a girlfriend before you left for America, that isn't Shar but is someone else? Were you running away from the breakup?"

"No. Well, I suppose a bit. She wanted to get married and I didn't. I wanted to see more of the world."

This was all too much.

"Does she live here?"

"Yes."

"Will she want to stab my eye out, like Shar?"

"No, I don't think so. Honestly, Tilda, I don't think it was me she was in love with. It was the idea of being married and having a family. She found a nice guy and I think she's happy with him. It also helps that she isn't barking mad, like Shar Mahoney."

"Mama, can we go to the park now? Deacon says there's a park close that we can walk to." Logan, who I just realized had been sitting in the room the entire time, had clearly bored of this drama. Thankfully, he was in headphones for most of the conversation.

"Of course, buddy. Have you guys brushed your teeth?"

"No." Logan just stood there.

"Um, can you guys go do that? And while you're

at it, Livia you need to brush your hair, baby."

If I was going to run into more girlfriends of Deacon's past, I wanted my kids to look like they were active members of society that didn't just crawl out of bed. I wasn't a neglectful mother. However, if someone were to judge me right now based on their breath and hair, it would be questionable.

Logan shouted from the upstairs bathroom, "I hate brushing my teeth! I don't even know where my toothbrush is!"

"It's in your suitcase!" I shouted from downstairs. Livia had already found her toothbrush and was halfway through her teeth brushing song.

"I don't know where my suitcase is!" Logan shouted again.

I looked at Deacon who seemed unfazed by this mind-numbing conversation. I needed to add a new item to my Bucket List...make it to 50 without pulling entire head of gray hair out.

I realized this conversation was going nowhere, so I found the toothbrush and toothpaste for Logan and reiterated the necessity of brushing one's teeth.

Once everyone's teeth were brushed, we left the house for the park. I was thankful the four us spent the hour there without a soul to disturb us. I didn't *not* want to meet people from Deacon's town. Quite the opposite really. Everyone I met so far, aside from Shar, was lovely. The stress of meeting his fake ex-girlfriend, anticipation of meeting his mother, and possibly his real ex-girlfriend was beginning to take its toll. I needed to figure out a way to decrease my anxiety.

We quietly watched the kids play on the playground equipment when Deacon said, “It seems the walk this morning didn’t give you a break. Why don’t you take a nice bubble bath and relax? I can hang out with the kids while they play.”

“I don’t think I have any bubble bath and it probably wouldn’t help.”

“You do have bubble bath because I brought some with me in my bag. There’s also a candle in the bathroom and some champagne chilling in the fridge.”

“How did you do that without me noticing?”

“When your love is jet lagged from a long journey it’s not too difficult. Now go. We’ll be back in a bit. They’ve met some new friends over there, and I don’t think I’ve kissed that lady so it’s all good.” He gave me a kiss and sent me on my way.

I walked back to the house, trying to think of the last bubble bath I took and realized I couldn’t remember.

It felt weird to be in the rental house all alone, but I followed Deacon’s instructions and found the champagne in the refrigerator and took it upstairs to the bathroom. To the side of the clawfoot tub, sat a bottle of bubble bath, candles, matches and a champagne glass waiting for me. I poured the champagne into the glass, lit the candles and poured the bubble bath into the running warm water. Stepping into the bath, I took a deep breath for relaxation. It was absolute delight to simply lay back and enjoy the peace and quiet… the champagne didn't hurt the serenity either.

I thought about how my husband, in all our years of marriage, never did anything like this for me. Not even in the early wooing stages before kids and mortgages. Steve was kind and supportive in the beginning of our relationship, just not overly romantic. As time went on, he became even less thoughtful. Less caring. I think by the end, the small acts of kindness he once showed disappeared, I assumed I wasn't deserving of them. I wasn't good enough. Little did I know, he was saving those small, romantic acts for someone else.

I listened to a bit of my favorite self-help audio book and resolved I was good enough. Good enough to meet any of the women in Deacon's life. Good enough to have love and good enough to enjoy a night out sans children. At least after 9:00 at night. I hoped my *Good Enough* mantra was strong enough to hold through this evening.

We all hung around the house and relaxed for a bit after my calming bath. In the kitchen, Deacon taught Logan how to make a cup of tea with the electric kettle while in the living room, Livia made a new Lego creation from a set Deacon picked up at the local toy store.

Since Deacon was working tonight, he left for the pub earlier than we did. I figured I would walk with the kids down to the Stags Leap around 7:00

pm. That gave them plenty of time to hang out, eat and be my buffers in case any conversation got awkward or uncomfortable.

Good enough. I am good enough. They are just women. My insecurities were in full force tonight and I wasn't sure why. Maybe it was because I loved Deacon and I didn't want any reasons to leave him, like a mother who hated me.

When we entered the pub, Deacon, with his guitar in hand, was getting ready to go on. I had only seen him play a couple of times, but each time he gave me even more butterflies. When Deacon sang, his blue eyes got brighter. His fingers strummed his guitar gracefully and then there was his voice. His voice was so full of emotion and candor.

The kids and I found seats near the back of the room and listened to him. Some of his music was fast but more of it was slow and about love. The losses and feelings of love. I looked over to see the kids genuinely excited to listen to him. They were proud.

When Deacon finished his second song, he took a quick break and came over to greet us. I was so mesmerized by him, that when he walked over it took me a second to realize he was coming over to me.

On his way to greet me, another woman that wasn't Doris stopped him with a tray of drinks and motioned to take them over to a nearby table. He looked over at me and mouthed, 'sorry' as he delivered the pints to his patrons.

I watched the woman talk to the customers as she maneuvered through crowds, pouring drinks. It seemed natural, almost like dancing. I decided her dark blonde hair, blue eyes and chin dimple were no coincidence. This was Deacon's mother.

I hoped I wasn't staring too much.

I was staring too much. As I quickly looked away, I saw her pointing to me and talking to Doris. Dammit Aunt Beebie. Why didn't you have lip reading as one of the things on your bucket list?

"Mommy, can I have more Coke?" Livia asked, in the midst of scooping her ketchup off the plate with her fingers. According to my daughter, ketchup is most definitely a food group.

"No, baby. I think you've had enough soda today. How about some water?"

"Can I have more Coke?" Logan asked.

"As if I'm going to let you have some and not your sister. No."

Honestly, I needed a refill as well, but mine wasn't going to be just soda this time. I was terribly nervous and uncomfortable. I decided it was time to take my insecurities into my own hands. I was going to the bar to get a drink and some fresh water for my children. I mean, their hydration was at risk. I could do this.

I boldly stood up and said to the kids, "Stay here. I'm going to get us some more drinks."

"Cokes! Get us Cokes!" Logan shouted in one last attempt at his sugar and caffeine fix.

The pub had gotten quite busy, but I found

a spot at the bar. Doris turned around. Dammit Doris. I've already met you.

"Well hello, love. What can I get ya?"

"Hi Doris. Can I get a rum and coke for me and a couple bottles of water for the kids? Oh hell, and a couple more cokes. They're on vacation."

"Of course. Go have a seat. I'll have Mary bring your drinks to you. I think your Deacon is about to sing again." She smiled and took my money.

"Mama, did you get us drinks?" Logan asked when I got back to our table.

"Yes, they're coming. It's quite busy tonight you know. People must be here to listen to Deacon."

Logan observed thoughtfully and said, "He sounds like someone that would be on the radio."

"You're right. He does. Who knew our Deacon was so talented?"

"I've known my Deacon was a talent since he was a lad." Mary had arrived with our drinks. "You must be the lovely, Tilda Loxley. I'm Mary. Mary Kelly."

"It's so nice to finally meet you. I know we spoke a bit on the phone one day. It's nice to actually meet you, meet you." Oh lord. I was rambling like a nervous nelly.

Although Deacon's mother didn't tower over me, she was taller than me and much slimmer. Almost too slim. The kind of slim that seems like she works more than eats. I imagined the stress of her husband's illness probably didn't help. She had a kind face, much like her son's but it was far more tired than I'd ever seen Deacon's.

"I wish I could talk more Tilda, but we're very busy tonight. I have tomorrow off. I'd like to have you and the children over for dinner."

It was loud, I could barely hear her. I shouted back over the noise, "That sounds wonderful." My relationship with Deacon had officially evolved. I was having dinner with the parents.

"I'll let Deacon know what time later." Mary smiled and then hurried back to the bar.

Maura Kelly came over to the pub around 8:30 pm and sat with the kids and me for a few minutes before taking them back to the house to get them ready for bed. I had set out their pajamas and toothbrushes before we left to make their bedtime routine easier for everyone.

Deacon and I walked home once his shift was over. It was one of the first moments in a while that we'd been able to relax and enjoy one another's company.

"So, my mum invited us over for dinner tomorrow?"

"That's what she said. How do you feel about that?"

"What do you mean? I love it. You can finally get to know my family without having Patrick "Loudmouth" O'Toole in your ear. That man has got to get a job. He's in the pub every day!"

"Do we need to bring something? Like wine or something? Or flowers?"

"Ah, that's nice. Let's bring my mum some

flowers. It's probably been twenty years since my dad's done that. Shit, I shouldn't talk bad about him. He's a good guy. He brings my mum a cup of tea every morning before she gets out of bed."

I could see the look on Deacon's face, remembering his father's health was so poor. Honestly, though, you wouldn't think it if you didn't know the man. The doctor might say he was on death's door, but he refused to give up his work at the pub.

"Sooo, the kids will likely be asleep when we get home..." I said, trying to change the subject for Deacon.

We walked into the house, to find Maura asleep on the sofa. The kids were presumably in their bunk beds. I gently touched her shoulder.

"Oh, hi, sorry, I fell asleep. The kids got to sleep about an hour ago. I think they're still a bit jet lagged."

"Thank you so much for watching them for me. I hope they weren't any trouble. How much do I owe you?" I pulled out my purse to get some Euros for her.

"Tilda, we're family. We don't charge family." Deacon said, firmly.

"Are you sure? Maura dropped everything to help me out tonight. I'd like to give her something."

Maura got up to leave and said, "It's okay Ms. Loxley. I didn't have any plans. The kids were great. Much better than the little brats down the street I take care of. I'll see you later. Let me know if you need anymore help Ms. Loxley. Bye!"

I followed her to the door.

"Shhhh." I whispered. Her eyes got wide, and she smiled broadly. Family or not, her time was valuable, and I appreciated her help.

"I saw that Tilda. You just made that girl's week."

"Well, I was a teenager once. A hundred years ago."

"Oh Tilda Loxley. You are the sexiest and most beautiful hundred-year old I know."

We laughed as he pulled me close and kissed my neck. Then he pulled down my shirt a bit to kiss my shoulder as his hands went up from the bottom of the shirt to gently squeeze my breasts. Then we went upstairs to finish what we had so clearly started.

Chapter 17

The kids woke up at their typical time, around 8 in the morning, which meant the jet lag had finally subsided. Of course, in a few days, they would have it again.

Feeling some anxious about being with Deacon's family this afternoon, I decided to try my hand at a run. People in movies do it all the time. Run that stress away. Those people probably didn't have two kids though and don't need to wear Depends for a light jog. Nevertheless, I persisted.

Despite my light bladder leakage, I was beginning to enjoy running. I could pop some buds in my ear and be in my own head. I also felt like I needed to take a shot at an actual long-distance run. I still wasn't sure if Aunt Beebie would consider a 5K as long distance. So often, I wished she were here to talk to.

She might say, *Tilda push yourself more. You can do it*. Or she might say, *Tilda, don't let a little LBL keep you from your fitness goals. Everyone pees their pants sometimes.*

Oh, Aunt Beebie.

It was cold this morning. The pathways were damp from a recent rain and the air was still misty. I kind of liked it. If I were forced to choose heat or cold, I would choose cold in a heartbeat. Maybe I was cut out for Ireland after all?

My fitness tracker told me I'd nearly completed

three miles by the time I made it back to the rental house. Thankfully I didn't get lost. A lot of the houses and streets looked similar, but my route was straightforward. My mind felt clearer and my anxiety had all but diminished. Only to be replaced by wretched body odor. Not so sexy.

"Hi guys! I'm back. Gonna take a quick shower!"

The clawfoot tub had a long stand to hold the hand shower and I debated before finally deciding on a soak instead of a shower. I loved how European bathrooms always had hand-held shower heads and resolved to investigate an install when we got back home. Once the bath was filled with warm water, I got into the tub.

I heard a soft knock on the door, assuming it was one of the kids. Although, they typically just barge in, forgoing any ideas of privacy.

"Come in." I groaned.

But it wasn't the kids. It was Deacon.

"What are you doing?" I asked, embarrassed that my kids might see him sneaking into my bathroom.

"Don't worry. They're watching Netflix on their iPads...with headphones."

I was at the mercy of a twenty-eight-year old's libido, not to mention my newfound drive for affection. So, I gave in and let him in the oversized tub with me to continue our pleasure in great depth.

Deacon snuck out to our room to get dressed while I dried off in the bathroom. I couldn't believe

I had sex in a bathtub. Steve never would have been interested in anything remotely spontaneous, at least not with me.

We spent the rest of the morning hanging out with Logan and Livia before we prepared ourselves for the afternoon at Deacon's parents. The kids weren't happy about leaving the house, much preferring wi-fi and cartoons. We both assured them however, that the Kelly's were active in this century and could provide a wi-fi password to ease their iPad separation anxiety.

Since it was raining quite hard, Deacon drove us to his parent's home. We stopped at a corner shop to pick up some wine, which I insisted on, and some pretty flowers. I don't know anybody who can turn their nose up at a beautiful bouquet of lilies.

We pulled up to his parent's house and I held the flowers and wine as Deacon helped the kids out of the car. I was still a bit anxious and wanted something to present to his mother besides a nervous smile. The lilies smelled wonderful in the cool, Irish summer rain.

Deacon walked us into his home and I quickly handed the floral arrangement to Deacon's mother, while his father took the wine. Except instead of the anticipated glee I imagined, she simply looked at them in horror and began to sneeze profusely. Perhaps even violently. It was a disaster.

"Oh, my goodness. I am so sorry, Mary," I said, cringing from embarrassment.

"It's fine, love. You weren't to know I have an extreme allergy to pollen. Now, my son on the other hand..." Mary Kelly said, wiping her swollen, red nose and glaring at Deacon.

"Ma, I'm sorry. That's why Dad never gives you flowers. I remember now."

"Oh, so you thought all this time I was a sorry sack who didn't romance your mother?"

Deacon's brother-in-law, Donno thought this whole conversation was hilarious.

"Fuck off, Donno. You haven't given my sister anything but the Clap."

"Deacon Kelly! You take that back! I've never had the Clap!" Deacon's sister yelled from the nearby kitchen.

"That's not what I heard." Deacon continued to provoke his still black-eyed brother-in-law.

Donno stood up and said, "Do you want another broken nose? You piece of shit."

"Enough! That's enough! We have children present!" Deacon's mother was having none of this, probably because she knew where it would lead.

I sat there watching silently, still highly embarrassed our flowers gave Mary Kelly an asthma attack. And, I was fascinated by what was happening and wanted to know what would happen next.

The kids, however, were oblivious because James Kelly had given them the wi-fi password upon arrival. My two little zombies were in the zone. This time, I was thankful.

I could hear Deacon's sister prepping in the kitchen, avoiding it all. I popped my head around the corner and said, "Orla, can I help you in the kitchen?"

Deacon's sister looked relieved. "Yes, that'd be lovely, Tilda." She elegantly chopped the carrots and turnips before adding them to the roast pan. "Will you chop the onions for me?" Orla handed me a bowl of onions and moved a paring knife over my way.

"Orla is a beautiful name. Is it a traditional Irish name?" I asked, peeling and chopping the onions, desperate to not ruin my eye makeup.

"Yes, it is. My mum planned on calling me Ciara, but when I came out, my blonde hair screamed *Golden Princess*. So, I'm Orla. Does your name have meaning?"

"Well, I was born Matilda. My mother always called me Tilda though, so I'm Tilda."

"I think we forget how much of an impact our mothers have in our lives. Does your mum live close?"

"Oh, um, no." I hated this part. "My mom died quite some time ago. And my dad died when I was a child...so, it's just me."

"Oh, Tilda, I'm sorry."

"It's okay. It's not your fault. I've gotten quite used to it now. I had a support system. My great Aunt Beebie was a big help when I was young. I suppose that's why her Bucket List is so important to me."

"Bucket List?"

"Oh, I guess Deacon didn't mention it? It's kind of how we met. Anyway, she had a Bucket List that didn't get finished and, in her will, she asked me to do complete it for her. I'm nearly done."

"What things have you done so far?"

"I took a trip with the kids to see the Northern Lights, I went to Venice with Deacon, where we had an awful falling out. I'm taking a dance class and teaching an English class. They're both quite fun. I still have a few things to do though. Like pose nude for an art class. Not looking forward to that one."

Orla nearly spit out her wine.

"Yes, that's typically everyone's reaction. Especially if you knew how much I hate being naked."

"I don't mean to judge, but who puts that on a bucket list? That's hilarious!"

"My Aunt Beebie was an interesting lady. Full of surprises."

"Well, good for you, Tilda. Don't let my brother hold you back from it all. He'd have you pregnant and hanging out in the pub your whole life if he could."

I found her comment interesting, because I never got the impression Deacon was remotely interested in that type of life.

"I think I'm too old for that, I'm afraid."

"What? No, you aren't." She obviously didn't know how old I was.

"Orla, I'm forty. That's too old for kids."

"You might think you are, but Deacon probably

doesn't. I assumed Donno didn't really want to have kids. Then I got knocked up on the honeymoon and the rest is history. We have four kids now and we couldn't be happier."

"I'll talk to him about it. Thanks for the advice."

"So how does your Bucket List have anything to do meeting Deacon?"

"Oh, Aunt Beebie wanted to kiss a stranger with reckless abandon." I smiled, thinking about our first night, as hazy as it was.

"I heard my name. What are you ladies discussing?" Deacon came up behind me and wrapped his arms around my waist. "The kids are asking for you. I think they want some of that crack drink, Coke is it?" He laughed. My kids had obviously taken their vacation beverages to an extreme.

"We have some Cokes and waters in the fridge for them. Dinner won't be for a bit. Deacon bring them all out some crisps and waters. If that's okay, Tilda?"

"Yes, of course. Thank you."

Since I wanted to check on them, I carried the snacks out with Deacon, pleased to find they had finally put down their electronics to play different electronics with Orla's kids. At least they were socializing, I thought. However, once we got back to reality, I needed to have an iPad detox plan set for them.

Deacon's mother came out from the kitchen, bringing more treats out for the kids. "I'm sorry about that mess from Deacon and Donno, Tilda.

They've always been at each other's throats. Like brothers they are. Do you have any siblings?"

"No, unfortunately I was an only child." When I was a kid, I wished for a sibling every night. Once my dad got sick, I knew it would never happen. My mother got me a cat once though.

"Orla and Deacon fight but they love each other. I think." She laughed, picking up some trash from the first round of the kids' snacks.

"I'm sure they do. If you can't fight with your siblings and know they'll still love you, then you can't fight with anybody."

We walked to the back of the room with our drinks and sat down. I felt like I was about to have the talk.

"So, what do you and Deacon have planned?" She asked with a strain on her face.

"I guess it's all very irresponsible. I don't know. I never planned any of this. Falling in love. Him going back to Ireland. We've been avoiding a serious conversation about it, I'm afraid. Do you disapprove? Of us?"

How was I so bold? Was it the second glass of wine? Why would I even ask such a question??

"Deacon loves you with all his heart. I know that. I've never seen him like this with another woman. But that's what frightens me a bit. A mother never wants to see her son hurt."

There it was. Despite the graciousness, she was still a mother. I understood completely.

"No, I don't want to see any of us hurt. The kids

absolutely adore him, Mary. I don't know what to do. I sincerely don't. There are a lot of hearts at stake."

"I know you know that, love. Just be thoughtful about it all. The right decision will come to you."

I had a feeling she knew what the right decision was, but I knew she wasn't going to share it with me.

If only I could read minds as well as lips!

We had our dinner and socialized about our lives a bit before heading back to the rental.

"Tilda, did Deacon tell you what a wonderful football player he was as a lad? He made the city team you know." Mary said, passing the roast potatoes to James.

"He mentioned it once, but I didn't know you made the city team, Deacon!" He was my dream fella. A footballer and musician.

"Bah, it was nothing. I blew out my knee the first week. Doctor said I shouldn't play anymore."

"That's what led him to his music. He couldn't impress the ladies anymore with his football legs." Orla laughed.

James added, "I for one am happy he plays his music more. Brings more ladies to the pub. Sorry, Tilda. No disrespect."

"None taken. I'd come to the pub more often as well. I love Deacon's music."

"Me too." Livia said, between bites of bread. "His music should be on the radio."

"Spare me." Donno said, quietly, as Orla kicked

him under the table and Livia shot him a look of disdain. "Sorry, love. Just not my type of music, is all. I like something a bit less lovey dovey. Like Ozzy Osbourne. Don't hear him crying all the time do ya?"

"Donno, Livia doesn't listen to Ozzy Osbourne. Right, dear?" Mary asked.

"Oh, we listen to him sometimes on the way to school!" Logan replied.

Donno laughed, while Mary looked at me in shock.

I cleared my throat, embarrassed, "Sometimes we like something to get our energy up in the morning."

We quietly finished our dinner and said our goodbyes for the evening.

Heading home in the car, I wondered if this was what life would be like had we lived here. Weekend dinners at his parents, helping his sister in the kitchen while the two men duked it out in the living room.

"Penny for your thoughts, Tilda." Deacon asked as we got ready for bed.

"Your mom is worried you'll be hurt. That I'll hurt you."

"My mum worries about everything. She likes you though." He said sliding under the sheets.

"I don't know. I think she's suspicious of me."

"She's not suspicious. She wants you to come and stay here. For good."

"What?! No, I don't think so. She'd probably

prefer you stay here and marry that girl who loves you."

"Definitely not. She knows as well as you do that Shar Mahoney is mad as a hatter. We have enough of that in our family."

"I'm serious though. I'm worried about what we're going to do. The kids and I leave in a few days and we're no closer to figuring out our relationship. You can't leave your family. They clearly need you. Logan and Liv start school soon. Once that begins, I can't pick up and leave." I started to cry at this point. The whole thought of our conundrum left me extremely emotional.

"Hey, hey, don't cry. We will figure it out. I've told you. I love you and we will figure this out."

"Ok." I said, wiping the tears off my freshly moisturized face. "Do you want me to come here and stay? For good?"

Deacon sighed and said, "Of course. This is my home. But I also know that's not an easy decision. I tried to start a new life in the States, and it didn't go so well. Ah, I take that back. Some of it went perfectly well."

He kissed my forehead and held me in his arms until I fell asleep.

We spent the last few days enjoying life in Deacon's town. Hanging out at the pub. Playdates with Orla's kids. Maura even came over to babysit while Deacon and I had a quiet dinner out. The kids and I were so comfortable it was difficult to accept we were leaving.

There was a heavy feeling in the air. I scheduled our driver to pick us up rather than have Deacon take us to the airport. I wanted to say our final goodbyes at the house, preferring time to compose myself on the drive to the airport.

"You'll call me when you get home?" Deacon asked, teary eyed at the thought of us leaving.

"Yes. Although I don't know what time it will be here."

"No need to worry. I'll be waiting no matter the time. Just let me know you made it back safely."

We had a long kiss, followed by hugs with the kids and a couple extra hugs with each other after that. Once the kids and I were driving away, I looked back, waiting for him to go walk away, but he didn't. He stood there on the lonely street watching us drive away.

While we drove to the airport, I sat quietly, thinking about Deacon, about us. Normally, after a long trip away from home, I find I am excited to get back to our normal. Normal bedtimes, normal meals, normal schedules. I wasn't excited to head back home this time though. I was devastated to have to leave Deacon. I didn't know when I could see him again and that terrified me.

I knew the kids hated saying goodbye to him as well. They loved spending this week with Deacon. Getting up with him in the mornings. Having an extra grown up help them with breakfast and even little things like pouring milk. We played house and I felt guilty tearing them away from it.

We spent a couple of hours at the airport waiting for our plane. I called Cassie to let her know we were scheduled to leave soon. She'd taken us to the airport and insisted on picking us up. I was grateful she answered her phone. I needed someone to talk to about my anguish over leaving Deacon.

"Ah Tilda, I'm sorry this is so hard. I know there isn't an easy answer."

"I'm having a really hard time saying goodbye to him this time. I think I've really fallen, Cassie."

"Well, what did you think of Ireland? How is James?" James was Cassie's cousin from her mother's side. Her mother married an American businessman and the rest was history. Most of her family still resided in Ireland.

"He didn't look well, but he moved around and acted as though he were in perfect health."

"That's typical James from what I remember. I need to take a trip back there, myself. It's been several years. Did you get along okay with Mary?"

"I think so. Deacon said she liked me, but I don't know. She basically told me she was worried I'd break her son's heart."

"Yikes."

"Yeah. Yikes is right. It was so awkward, yet I totally get it."

"Oh! I'm totally changing the subject here, but I think I found a way for you to check another bucket list thing off! I was talking to this lady who works at the community center. She has an art class for seniors. She's willing to let you do the nude thing."

"Are you serious?"

"Yes. I'll text you her info. Isn't that exciting? I thought you'd be more excited. You're almost done!"

"Yeah… no, I'm not excited about the nude part, but I am excited to be closer to finishing Aunt Beebie's Bucket List."

I lied. Not about the nude part, that was clearly not exciting. But I wasn't really excited about finishing the list. The list was a way for me to reconnect with my long-lost Aunt. It was the beginning of my relationship with Deacon.

I didn't want it to be the end as well.

Chapter 18

Getting home helped my overall anxiety and after a couple of weeks, I felt even more settled. Life was busy. August was in full force. In Ireland, I didn't have places to be or important things to do. Once I got home, I had a lot of places to be and important things to do. There were last minute school forms to fill out, first day of school outfits to choose, backpacks to fill with school supplies.

The English classes were still commencing, and not to brag, but I think I was teaching some excellent English. Shira, my Israeli student was swearing far less. I hadn't heard an F bomb from her in at least two classes. She still got aggravated with Omar though. There wasn't anything to prevent that. Poor Omar. His pronunciations of English words were vastly improving, despite Shira's fussing at him.

JoJo, my student from China, also improved greatly. She was able to introduce herself, recite numbers 1-100 and have a basic conversation. Granted, we always had the same conversation. I told myself she just liked to ask people how their day was every week.

Manuel was my most improved. He not only learned his numbers, colors and basic conversation skills, he was able to quote his favorite television shows from the previous night. He did an excellent impression of George Costanza from

Seinfeld.

Besides the English class I taught, my dance class was also keeping me busy. Our recital was in a few weeks. Kyle's confidence was much improved thanks to his engagement. It was as though all fear was dissolved once his lady, Sarah said yes.

Ms. Bolivar clapped her hands and said, "Wonderful dancing tonight, class! I will see you all next week."

Kyle and I walked over to the bench, both glowing from perspiration, due to the demands of our tiny, but demanding dance teacher.

"I can't wait for your family to see how far you've come, Kyle. When you dance at your wedding, they'll be amazed, I think. Not that you were terrible."

"It's okay, Tilda. I was terrible. I've never been coordinated. You've helped a lot." Kyle said as he put away his dancing shoes and slid his sneakers on. "I meant to ask you, if you wanted to come to our engagement party. I had an actual invitation, but I lost it. I can text you the info though. It's in a couple of weeks."

"Kyle, that is so sweet. I'd love to. I'll just have to check and make sure I don't have anything else going on."

"Sure, I understand."

I was positive I didn't have anything going on. My social calendar had become rather quiet lately. Cassie was busy dealing with her divorce and Tabitha was on one last getaway before school started next week. I was shocked how fast the summer went by.

I was also shocked to think I'd been working on this bucket list for almost a year and I still had things to complete.

I had held onto the contact information Cassie gave me for the art class lady, Rose for about two weeks before sending her an email. Of course, she responded right away. Apparently, the class had been going on for a few weeks, but she still had a need for one more model. I had two weeks to psych myself up for my first nude model session.

The two weeks went by entirely too quickly.

I walked into the building and found the classroom where the art class took place.

"You must be Tilda! I'm so glad you were able to make it." Rose greeted me as I walked into the empty room. She set up the "changing room" which was a room divider panel to give me privacy while I disrobed and slipped on the thin robe hanging on the divider.

"Each week, the class observes a different model and uses different materials." My week, she said was charcoal.

"That's the most flattering, in my opinion." Rose said. "And don't worry. The students are extremely professional. This isn't pornography by any means. Imagine yourself as a Florentine sculpture."

I imagined myself running away to a five-star Florentine hotel as I reluctantly walked over to spot where the model poses.

"How does this work? Do, I just sit however?" I asked, trying to maneuver myself in a way where the entire class didn't see my lady parts. I've had two kids. Nobody needs to see that.

I felt so clueless. I'd never taken a real art class before. Not even art history. Anything that had to do with drawing or creating anything artistic for that matter, I avoided. Not because I don't like art. On the contrary. Art doesn't like me.

"You'll be sitting for over an hour so find yourself a comfortable pose. I've fixed the thermostat, so you won't freeze from the air conditioning. The poor fella last week suffered terribly."

"Suffered terribly?!"

"Well we had that cold front come through. The thermostat couldn't keep up with it, and all this crazy weather. It was an igloo in here. Even the class complained. One lady said her work was ruined from her nose dripping all over it. I'm not sure that's even possible but what do I know, right?" Rose said while she dusted off some chairs, preparing for the arrival of my artists.

There was no way I was getting out of this. My heart pounded. I could feel sweat dripping down my arm. My head began to feel warm. I thought I would pass out at any moment. Then, from out of nowhere I heard a voice. I must have been imagining, of course. But that voice. I knew that voice.

Snap out of it. You can do this, Tilda. It's just a

bunch of old fogeys finding something to do besides Bingo. They don't care about your lady parts.

But what if they think I'm gross?

It's not about what they think. It's about what you think, my dear.

That was when I got it. I understood why Aunt Beebie put something as crazy as posing nude for an art class. It was a way for her to accept herself. To literally, feel comfortable in her own skin.

The class had settled in their seats and were so quiet I would be able to hear a pin drop. This was my moment. I took a deep breath and removed the light robe. The spotlight shone down on me in all my glory.

As the artists worked, the only sound in the room was charcoal sticks and pencils scratching up against their paper. I may have heard a fart from somewhere, but I guess it may have been a chair. Who knows, maybe art is like yoga.

I looked at the clock, hoping the hour was nearly over. My neck had begun to spasm from the way I was holding my head. Alas, we were only halfway through. To distract myself from the neck pain, I thought of Deacon.

I wondered what he was doing. It was late at night in Dublin. Maybe he was sitting in the pub with his guitar. I imagined being there, hearing his voice and guitar sail through my ears. He sang with such sincerity and emotion. I missed his voice. Hearing his strong fingers strumming the guitar strings. He was incredibly talented with so much life to explore. Why would he want to waste it on me? An older woman with two, albeit fantastic, kids?

Darkness and doubt started to fog my memory of him.

"Okay class. That's it! Shall we thank our wonderful model, Tilda?" The class clapped, enthusiastically. I could hear people mumble to each other, words like— "beautiful," and "glorious." They may have been complimenting one another's artwork, but I chose to think the compliments were all about me.

The class ended a few hours before my dance class, so I rushed back home to spend some time with Logan and Livia. I always felt guilty anytime I was away from them for very long.

I stopped at Cassie's to pick up the kids.

"O hi Tilda. Come on in." Something wrong. Cassie is always upbeat and positive. She's even that way when she talks about her divorce, which says something.

"Is everything okay?"

Cassie looked to the back, where the kids were playing.

"My cousin James died this morning. His heart just gave out. I talked to Mary and she's just inconsolable. It's just awful."

"Oh my god. That's terrible. Did you talk to Deacon?" Shit. Deacon. I had my phone on silent from earlier. I rifled through my purse to find my phone.

He must have been trying to reach me.

But he hadn't. There were no missed calls or text messages. Nothing.

"I haven't spoken to him. Mary said he went off by himself and hasn't been back. I think he's taking it hard. They've closed the pub for a couple of days to focus on funeral arrangements. I think the wake is tomorrow."

"Cassie, I don't think I can go. The kids are starting school in a couple of days. I still have to buy backpacks and finish finding school supplies. I haven't found enough yellow folders! What am I going to do?"

"Tilda, it's okay. You don't have to do anything. Everyone is working on it there. You can't pick up and go to Ireland in a moment's notice. Deacon knows that."

She was right. I had responsibilities here, at home. But that didn't make me feel any less guilty for not being there for Deacon.

The pitfalls of a long-distance relationship.

"He hasn't texted me or anything. I don't know what to do."

Although I have dealt with plenty of death in my life, I still do not handle it well. I avoid funerals whenever I can. I stumble over my condolences and sometimes I even pretended like I had no idea it even happened. People probably assume I'm callous and uncaring, although that's not the case. My heart just doesn't know how to cope with it.

I wouldn't be able to ignore this though.

"Give him a call. If he doesn't answer, that's up to him. Just leave a message letting him know you're here to talk."

Cassie always knew the right things to say and do.

We rounded the kids up and I took them home. It was nearly dinner time. The babysitter would be here soon. I opted to make spaghetti. It was easy and the kids loved it.

While Logan and Liv watched television, I popped into the other room to call Deacon. He didn't answer, so I did what Cassie suggested and left him a message. It was awkward and uncomfortable. However, I was determined to let Deacon know I wasn't blowing off his father's death because I was unable to be there myself.

Maddie arrived as I finished making dinner. She helped get the kids to the table. I was out of red sauce but thankfully the kids didn't have any issues with parmesan and butter.

"Okay kids, I'm off to my dance class. Maddie, do you need anything before I head out?"

"Nope. I think we're good. Have fun at your class!" Maddie shouted from the kitchen, where she was preparing their drinks of water.

As usual, I was running a bit late. Kyle was already in his dance shoes when I arrived at class. In addition to his sweat and anxiety, he is very punctual.

I put my shoes on, silenced my phone, and resolved to spend the next hour focused on the tango. I was having trouble since it was such an emotional dance and my focus was on Deacon and his family. I also had two left feet. My dance partner somehow excelled throughout our class, while I stayed at a stagnant mediocre.

Still, mediocre was better than my skillset at the beginning of this journey. Positive thoughts, Tilda!

"Tilda, you seem out of sorts. What's up?"

"My friend Deacon's father died this morning. I feel bad that I can't be there for him."

"Listen to the music! Feel the music! The tango is an emotion!" Ms. Bolivar shouted over the music we all tried to feel.

"Your friend from the bar? I'm sorry. How sad. He's a good guy."

"That's it, Kyle! You're feeling the music! Keep up the good work for Tilda." Ms. Bolivar gently patted my back as she moved on to the other couples.

"I dare say you've met the approval of our dance instructor, young Kyle."

Kyle laughed, "That is the biggest surprise of my life. So, have you looked at your calendar for tomorrow night?"

"I did. I think I can come for a little bit. The kids are having a weekend with their grandparents before school starts so I have a bit of free time to myself."

"Good. I'm glad you can come. Sarah has about three times the family that I do, so every person helps. Oh, not that I invited you to be a body. I want you to be there. You helped me out so much when I had to talk to her father."

"How's that going by the way? Is he less scary?"

"Nope. Scarier. Now I'm responsible for his daughter's health and happiness."

"Well, I hope I can be of great support tomorrow night. Is the dress cocktail attire?"

"Yes."

"I'll pull something out of my closet."

"Thanks, Tilda."

Class finished and I rushed to my phone to see if Deacon had texted or called. But nothing. He still hadn't reached out to me.

I drove home wondering what I could do. But realistically, there was nothing I could do. My next thought process was to obsess if he was upset with me for not being there?

No, he knows my situation. He has always been understanding that I'm a single mom.

But this is different. His dad died. He would probably drop everything for me.

But he's not a single parent.

When I got home, I helped the kids get ready for bed. Next, I put my phone on the bedside table and tried not to think about it. If he wanted to talk to me then he would call.

After two episodes of The Crown, I finally fell asleep.

I woke up around 3:00 am to my phone ringing. It was Deacon, thankfully.

"I'm sorry I woke you."

"No, no it's fine. I'm glad you called. I'm so sorry,

Deacon. I was so worried about you."

"I know. I needed time alone. I wasn't trying to push you away. I just needed time to think."

"Of course. You know I'm paranoid, but I understand. I wish I could be there for you."

"I don't want to be away from you anymore, Tilda. If my dad's death has made me realize anything, it's that life is too short. Life is too short to worry about little things. You are the big thing."

My heart fluttered hearing him speak so beautifully. But I worried as well. Perhaps his current state of mind was somewhat responsible for his declarations.

"Oh Deacon, I love you. Just focus on your family right now. Okay? Don't worry about me. I'm not going anywhere. Well, except to Kyle's engagement party tomorrow night. Not looking forward to that to be honest."

"Kyle, from the pub? He got a yes from his lady, then?"

"Yep. I hear his proposal was quite romantic. He showed off his dance skills for her and everything."

"I bet I could beat him."

"Beat him? How so? Like beat him up?"

Deacon laughed, "No you daft woman. I could beat him in a romantic proposal."

This was the first time we had talked about *that*. Now I knew he was unstable in his emotions. Naturally, I pretended to ignore the comment and moved on.

"So, Cassie and her Erik are coming along with their divorce. It sounds like he doesn't want to take the house or anything. I don't think I've seen such a cordial separation."

"Well it's because he feels guilty."

"Why would he feel guilty? He said he didn't cheat. Did he cheat?! Do you know something?"

"What? No, I mean he feels guilty for being gay. I mean, it's obvious, right?"

Um. No. It was not obvious.

"Wait, you think he's gay? That never even occurred to me." It did make sense, now that I thought about it. I don't want to stereotype. Although he was a big Jennifer Lopez fan, and not for the booty. He also danced a little much when One Direction or Maroon 5 came on.

"But he hasn't told Cassie, I assume."

"No, she hasn't said anything to me. I'd think she knows I'm open-minded enough I wouldn't judge if he was. But I don't know for sure."

"Tilda, I have to go. I'm sorry. The priest is here to talk about my dad's wake. I'll call you later, okay? I love you.

"Love you, too. Bye."

Chapter 19

I got very little sleep, but I wanted to be up when the kids woke up to make them breakfast. Weekday mornings are usually frantic, and the kids mostly eat cereal or yogurt for breakfast. Weekends, however, are slower. The kids still get up at the same time, but they have time to get hungry and I have time to make pancakes and other homemade favorites. George likes it because Logan always sneaks bacon to her from under the table. George has such a great sense of smell and hearing that she can tell when a package of bacon opens from hundreds of feet away. It's rather impressive. This morning was no exception.

"You're not getting any bacon, George. Okay, maybe one bite." I said, breaking off a piece of freshly cooked bacon.

"Okay, kids. Come eat." I plated their food and brought it over to the table, with George following close behind.

"Mommy, I don't like bacon today." Livia said, scooting herself up to the table.

"Mom, I told Tyler I'd meet him at 9:00 outside to ride bikes."

"Logan, you need to finish your breakfast. Later we're driving to meet up with grandma and grandpa."

Logan took a bite of his bacon. "But mom we're working on a project! We have to finish it today!"

"Why today?"

"Because that's what we want to do! Please mom. I'm full."

"Logan, you just sat down! Eat." I said, annoyed that he wasn't more impressed with my fancy chocolate chip pancakes that were made with love.

"I want to go out and play too!" Livia added, piling pancakes into her mouth.

Logan took a bite of his pancakes and said, "No Livia. It's just me and Tyler."

"But I can help too!" Livia insisted.

"Logan, you can play with Tyler for a little while, but you have to check in with me at 9:30. You can't play all morning. We have other things to do."

Logan grumbled but agreed. "Fine."

"Livia, how about we play with your new doll? Or we can work on your comic? Or I know! You can help me pick out a dress for tonight? I'm going to a party for a friend. I don't even have an idea what to wear. I really need your help, Livia."

I also wanted to be up early to have an idea what I was wearing to the cocktail party. I wasn't excited to go alone. I also wasn't excited to try on all my dresses from the back of the dusty closet. Thankfully my exercising should mean I could still fit in the old dresses from back in the day.

Livia and I went upstairs to my closet where she picked out a comfortable, yet classy little black dress. I never wore dresses anymore unless it was a summer maxi dress that flowed and showed no rolls.

"Good choice, Livia."

"I think you wear a lot of black, but I like this one. It's pretty. I like the lacy skirt part." Livia provided her opinion and proceeded to walk out of the closet and into my bedroom to draw. I always have a broad assortment of toys, markers and coloring books in my bedroom.

"Hmm." I remembered the last time I wore this dress. It was a work function of my late husband's. Although I haven't weighed myself recently, I felt confident I had lost weight since then.

"Hmmm."

My contemplation was interrupted to solve an important crisis of why Livia's pen wouldn't work on the paper she wanted to draw on. Then it turned into a crisis of why she couldn't figure out how to draw SpongeBob today and so on and so forth.

"Livia, what about this dress? Do you like it?"

She sobbed, "I don't care about your dress. I want to draw now, and I can't!"

"Okay. Can I help? Let's try a new piece of paper and pencil." I went to my bedside table to find a pad of paper and luckily, a freshly sharpened pencil. With a little assistance, Livia drew her rectangle and the rest of SpongeBob.

Once that crisis resolved, Logan was upset because he still wanted to go ride his bike with his next-door neighbor friend, Tyler, who was waiting at the door. He couldn't come in because of his deadly allergy to dogs. Sometimes that works out fine for me because he doesn't have to see my messy house and then go home to tell his far more perfect mother what a hot mess I am. Anyway, Logan's tire needed to be pumped up and Logan could not find the pump. I found the pump in the box where the pump was supposed to go and thus another crisis was resolved.

Logan took a long breath and said, "Thanks, mom. I'm sorry I fussed at you."

I was shocked at his apology and simply said, "Logan, it's okay. Thank you for your apology. We all lose our tempers sometimes. Even me. Now, go play but stay out front so I can keep an eye on you. No adventures to the park."

"Okay. What time do I need to be back in?"

"We're leaving around noon to meet up with your grandparents. I want a check-in at 10:00 and you back inside for 11:30 so we can be ready to go."

Phew. I felt like Super Mom at that moment. I was also very tired from not sleeping well. So tired that while Logan was outside playing with his friends and Livia was playing dolls next to me, I fell asleep. So asleep, Livia had to shake me awake.

"Mama, I want some chocolate milk."

Wiping away my sleep slobber, I responded, "Huh? What? Oh, sure baby. I'll get you some." And then fell asleep for a second before Livia shook me awake one more time.

"Mama! I need chocolate milk!"

So much for being Super Mom.

I got Livia's chocolate milk and a granola bar

for snack, checked on Logan outside, who was creating an extreme version of hopscotch with his friends and then went back upstairs to figure out what to wear.

I went upstairs to try on one other dress that seem to have a little more room in different areas and worked for the occasion. It wasn't black, which is my go-to for any ensemble, but it was navy blue, close enough.

Since I wasn't going to see the kids for a couple of nights, and my in-laws weren't going to be able to make lunch, I wanted to take them for a quick meal. We stopped at Benny's Famous Burgers about halfway from our meeting point with their grandparents. Logan had his plain burger, while Livia had her non-burger with fries because some days, she refuses to eat meat. I guess this was one of those days. Livia pulled out her meat and placed it on Logan's plate, where he proceeded to add it to his plain single burger.

Given the cocktail dress disaster, I chose the green salad with a vinaigrette and bottled water. Terribly boring, given this place is known around the state for their delicious burgers and fries.

I let the kids get ice cream to eat on the rest of the trip, although only in a cup. I have learned my children, no matter their age, cannot eat ice cream cones. They and the ice cream have huge meltdowns, making a mess all over the car. So, no matter how much they plead, no ice cream cones in a car.

The goodbyes were quick for the kids, who were excited to see both grandparents. Now that they are older, goodbyes are more difficult for me than them.

The drive home was quiet until about halfway through when I suddenly got a terrible wave of nausea. I rushed to pull over to the side of the road where I proceeded to puke seconds after opening my car door.

"Oh great. This is how I'm going to die. E. Coli poisoning from eating lettuce instead of the burger!" I commiserated with myself.

Luckily, I still had my water and once I got whatever it was out of my system, I felt okay. Or did I? Things were slowly starting to add up. My nausea kicked in again, but for another reason.

No. No way. It's just the food and stress. That's it.

Just to make sure, I stopped at the CVS nowhere near my house to pick up a pregnancy test. Just holding it in my hand made me want to throw up.

Once I got home, the first thing I did was race to the bathroom to confirm that I had E. Coli poisoning from salad.

"Fuck." It wasn't poisoning at all. It was a plus sign on the pregnancy test indicator.

"Noooooooo!!!!" I cried. George, who had followed me in to the bathroom, wasn't sure what all the ruckus was about, but attempted to make me feel better with kisses.

This was not happening. My baby daddy lived in a different country and probably not prepared to be a husband or father. Dammit Deacon and his bathtub sex! This was all his fault. All of it. I was taking zero responsibility. Okay, maybe I had to take some, but I was blaming most of it on him.

I didn't know what to do. I wasn't ready to talk to Deacon. Not to mention he had plenty on his plate as it was.

My only option… call Cassie.

"Hey girl, what's up? I'm on my way to get groceries. Can I call you back?"

"Cassieeeeeeeeee. I'm pregnannnnnnnnnnt!!!!!" I squealed through tears.

"Holy shit. Hang on." I could hear Cassie pull over her minivan and take me off speaker. "Are you sure?"

"I just took a test. I thought all of my symptoms were early menopause. But then I puked on the way back from dropping off the kids, so I got a test. And it was positiiiiiive." I began to cry again.

"Well, I think it's wonderful. You love Deacon, and he loves you. This just solidifies where your relationship should be."

"Yeah but we don't know where we should be! We live in completely different countries! I can't live in a different country as my baby daddy!"

"Okay, first off, he's not your baby daddy. You make it sound like he was some one-night stand. That's not the case. Yes, your relationship is complicated. But you guys will figure it out. Can I be the godmother? I'm Catholic. I call dibs."

"Cassie, this is hardly the time to be calling dibs.

But yes, of course you'd be the godmother. But what am I going to do? I have this party to go tonight. Aw shit. I can't drink either."

God knows I needed a drink too. I wasn't ready for any of this. I was tired. I couldn't imagine being prepared for middle of the night feedings; of having to be on the schedule of an infant. I wouldn't have the help from grandparents I had with Logan and Livia. This baby's grandparent was in Ireland. They wouldn't have a relationship with my other children's relatives. Would they? All conversations I'd rather not have to have.

This was all too overwhelming.

"Tilda, just try to relax. It's going to be okay. Get ready for your party tonight, graciously turn down any wine due to you driving and try to enjoy yourself." Thank god for Cassie. "And don't worry about Deacon."

"Okay. Thank you for coaxing me away from the edge."

"Hey, you've coaxed me away from plenty of edges. I'm in the middle of a divorce. I'm sure I'll have some moments for you."

I asked Alexa to put on some fun music and tried to pump myself up for a good time tonight. I couldn't drink. I felt terribly stressed about my pregnancy news. I would go to the party, put on a brave face and pretend everything was perfectly normal.

Perfectly normal.

I put on my dress, did my makeup and as usual,

tucked my hair into a top knot because that was simple and cute. I also made sure to bring the ginger ale for sipping in the car on the way to the party. It seemed to help.

"Okay Tilda, you can do this." I pulled into the parking lot of the Country Club. The valet politely took my keys and handed me my ticket.

Now that I knew I was pregnant and not just bloated, I was painfully aware of all my symptoms. The heels I chose matched my navy dress but were the least comfortable in my closet. My extra control top undies were digging into my skin like they were a torture device from the Middle Ages. But hey, my nausea subsided after my pukes today. That was a bonus!

I spotted Kyle and Sarah in the middle of the room, chatting to an older couple. I didn't want to interrupt, so I meandered over to the table of crudités. Nothing says party animal like a lady munching on snap peas and ranch dressing.

As I drank my sparkling water and ate the tray of carrots and celery, a familiar face walked over to me. I knew this man, still I couldn't quite place him.

"You look very familiar. I don't know how, but I think we've met before." The dark-haired man said to me as he handed me another glass of sparkling water.

It took me a minute. Then it hit me. I knew exactly how I knew him. He was the photographer on our Northern Lights trip!

"How in the world? We met in Alaska! You're, wait, don't tell me. Um. Sam. Sam?"

He laughed and his eyes widened. "That's right! Tilda! How on earth did we end up at the same engagement party?"

"I don't know. I guess the fates knew I needed a buddy tonight. I don't know a soul here." I said as I munched on a baby carrot.

"Well, I know a lot of the people here. I'm Sarah's uncle. One of them. My sister was lucky enough to have five brothers."

"Do you live here?"

"To be honest, I travel so much I don't know where I live. But yeah, I have an apartment I rent, and my sister helps me keep an eye on things when I'm away."

"Have you had anymore travel adventures recently?"

"Well, I just got back from South America. It was hot and humid. Much like you'd expect. I had to sleep in a tent with mosquito nets and hope I didn't get malaria."

"They don't make you get vaccines for that?"

"Nah. It's more trouble than they're worth. My colleagues say they don't always work anyway."

"You might not feel that way if you get malaria."

"True. Thankfully I did not." Sam looked at my empty glass of water. "Can I get you anything else to drink? Wine or something?"

"Oh, uh, no thank you. I'm driving. I'd rather not risk it."

"Good thinking. I took a ride service. My family stresses me out and while alcohol may not be the best way to handle it, that is my treatment of choice." Sam said, grabbing a glass of merlot from a moving server's tray.

"No judgement here."

"Sam, I see you've met Tilda, my fabulous dance partner." Kyle said. He and Sarah had finally made it to our side of the room to greet us. Considering there must be 300 people here, I felt fortunate to be able to talk to them at all.

"What's this about dancing? Do tell Tilda." Sam replied with intrigue.

"There's not much to tell, Sam. One of my Bucket List items was to learn to dance. I joined a dance class, met Kyle here, who was trying to woo his Lady Love and here we are."

"Tilda has been a great support. They have a dance recital next week, in fact, and are dancing the Waltz and Tango." Sarah added to my abbreviated story.

"Well that's wonderful. I'd love to see your recital. Too bad I'm off to the Grand Canyon next week."

"Trust me, you are not missing a thing. No offense, Kyle."

"None taken, Tilda. We're a hot mess. Still, I'm proud of our progress. With that we must bid you adieu. There are another 200 people to talk to tonight. That's about half of our wedding guest list, by the way," Kyle said as he and Sarah moved on to their other guests leaving Sam and I alone again.

We chatted for a bit when I realized no one else was approaching Sam, their relative. "So, should I be concerned that nobody in your family is talking to you? Are you the black sheep, Sam? Has there been a prison sentence you haven't shared with me?"

Sam laughed, "No, no prison. I'm a divorced dad who doesn't see his kid enough and rents an apartment with not even a pet to call my own. They feel sorry for me. It's easier to just not talk to me."

"Well, I hate to disappoint you, but I think my pumpkin awaits me. I told Kyle I probably wouldn't stay too long. It was nice to talk to you again, Sam."

"You too, Tilda. It was nice to see you again."

I pulled the valet ticket from my purse and started to head out the door.

"Tilda, wait. Um, would you like to leave this place and go get coffee? I'd love an excuse to escape."

"Oh Sam, I'm sorry, I may have given you the wrong idea. I'm not really in place right now for, um..."

"No, I'm sorry. Just as friends. I have no business being in a, um, relationship. Anyway, there's a café around the corner that has a delectable tiramisu."

Shit. I can't eat tiramisu. Can I? It'd been so long since I'd been pregnant, I didn't know.

"Okay, sounds good. Let's go."

We walked around the corner to the café and chose one of their outside bistro tables. It all felt very European.

Sam ordered a cappuccino and tiramisu. I ordered a regular coffee and a croissant.

"Would you like to try it? It's truly the best tiramisu I've had in ages."

"Thanks, but no I can't eat it. It has alcohol in it." Aw crap. I said too much.

"Hmmm. Sparkling water, no dessert with alcohol." Sam pointed at me, "J'accuse!"

"Okay, Poirot, you've got me. I'm knocked up." I couldn't believe I said it out loud to a virtual stranger. My face turned warm and red at the realization.

"Sorry, it's none of my business."

"Well, it's rather complicated. The father lives in a town just outside of Dublin. He's 28, and works in a pub and plays a beautiful guitar and sings with a voice like butter."

"Ah. You haven't told him yet, have you?"

"How did you know? You really are Poirot."

"The shock on your face when you told me. Don't worry. Your secret is safe with me. But are you going to tell him?"

"Well of course. He's the father after all. It's a difficult time. We're apart, his father just died. I don't want to add to the confusion. I want him to be with me because of me. Not because I got pregnant."

"Okay. You seem to have it figured out for the time being."

"Yes, I suppose I do. But I should really be going.

I didn't sleep well last night, and this has been a dramatic day, with learning I'm knocked up and all."

"Absolutely. Consider this therapy session on me."

"I feel like all I did was talk about myself. I'm sorry. Next time I'll listen to your problems." Why did I say that? Next time? There shouldn't be a next time. I had no business having coffee with a single, incredibly handsome man in my current condition and love status.

What was my love status?

It was going to be another night of little sleep as I anxiously contemplated how to tell Deacon about the pregnancy and discuss our future together. Or not together?

Chapter 20

The kids were back at school, thus missing out on my "mid-morning" morning sickness. Still, I was having a difficult time hiding my pregnancy symptoms from them. I had 'The Flu' now for a week— with no other ailments besides needing to run to the bathroom every once in a while.

I had to go to the September PTA meeting this morning. I was absolutely dreading it. It wasn't because Tabitha Wells was an evil bitch. She was my friend, now. However, feeling like I might actually be the color green didn't help my volunteer mojo.

"I'm sorry, you guys, I think I just ate something bad." I said to the group after the second run to the teacher's restroom.

"Or you could just be pregnant." One of Tabitha's cronies laughed. Not funny Mindy. Not. Funny.

Tabitha agreed. "No, no. We like Tilda now, Mindy so I need you to stop being a mean girl or you'll be on the next list." Tabitha said with a nonchalant laugh. Mindy, not sure if Tabitha was joking or serious, just followed along with nervous laughter.

When the meeting ended, Tabitha walked out with me.

"So was Mindy, right?"

"Huh? Oh, is it that obvious?"

"Well, I suppose you could have food poisoning. But you have that, *I'm pregnant and feel like shit* appearance."

"Wonderful. I guess I'm not doing a very good job at hiding it."

"Want to go get some breakfast? Oh wait, probably not."

"Actually, I need some protein. And pancakes. I definitely need pancakes."

"Perfect. Me too. Protein that is. Not pancakes. Yuck." Of course, Tabitha Wells doesn't eat pancakes. That's how she has a butt you can bounce a quarter on, and I have a butt you could land a fighter jet on. Okay, slight exaggeration. But that's how I feel when I'm around her.

We arrived at the restaurant and once we were seated, I ordered a juice, coffee, bacon, pancakes, hash browns and scrambled eggs.

"I don't plan on eating everything, don't worry. I'm not going to gain my nine months weight in one week. I just can't decide so I ordered everything."

"It's none of my business. But I have to ask. Is this the result of your Irish romance?"

"Well since he's the only romance I've had lately, yes, it is. I still need to tell him. I just haven't figured out when and the best way. I really don't want to tell him over the phone."

"True. It's not everyday conversation. But when do you see him next? The last I heard you guys were up in the air." Tabitha took a sip of her 'delicious' green drink.

"Well, his dad just died, and I haven't had a

chance to talk to him very much. He's basically running their family pub and helping his mom with everything. It's his birthday next week, but I doubt he'll be able to even celebrate."

I was excited he was turning 29. The closer he got to 30 the less I felt like a cougar. Unfortunately, Deacon turning a year old meant I was turning a year older.

Oh my god. I was going to be 41 and pregnant, without a husband. I needed more eye cream…and ketchup.

"Ma'am? Can I have ketchup for my hash browns? Oh, and some more cream for my coffee? Oh, and more coffee?" The server, after turning around twice just stopped and waited for me to add more items. "That's all. I promise. Thank you."

Tabitha stared at me in amazement.

"Wait when is your dance recital?"

"It's Saturday afternoon."

"It's too bad he can't come for that and celebrate his birthday at the same time."

"I know. I wish he could too."

I finished my breakfast, while Tabitha answered some messages from her personal training clients and finished her green drink.

"Well my friend, I must get to work. I have a client desperate to get into wedding dress shape for her upcoming nuptials. Keep me in the know with everything. I'll text you later to check in." Tabitha gave me a hug. "Don't worry, Tilda. I have a feeling that man of yours is going to be excited to start his new life with you. But you have to tell him first."

Why did everybody have to be so wise? I knew I had to tell him. I knew I would feel better if I told him. I just couldn't do it right now. I had an important Tango and Waltz to perform.

Saturday came before I knew it. The night before, Kyle and I put in an extra practice before my English class, since they're both in the same building. The kids tagged along for my practice and class keeping busy with schoolwork and play. They enjoyed watching us dance as well. Although, downloading instructional videos for extra help may have been a bad idea.

"Kyle, you need to put your back more back." Logan directed as he watched us and the video of the professional dancers.

"Mama, your feet shouldn't do that." Livia pointed down to my misplaced feet.

"Sorry, Kyle. My children have suddenly become Bob Fosse."

"It's okay. I think we needed this direction."

My little dance tyrants and I headed home after the rehearsal and English class, and I got them ready for bed. JoJo, my student from China had brought some dumplings and spring rolls for everyone. My kids won't eat most things I make for them, but JoJo's food they ate without a care in the world. They weren't hungry for dinner once we got home, but they did opt for a small bowl of cereal before bed.

I slept well that night, despite my nerves and excitement for the next day.

And then it came. The moment we'd all been waiting for. Our spectacular dance recital held at the glorious Ackerman Community and Senior Center.

Cassie arranged for a friend to do my hair and makeup, so I didn't have to worry about that part of the show. My long chestnut hair was tucked into a neat bun on top of my head, lavender eye shadow made my brown eyes pop. Thanks to a lovely stretchy material I stepped into my dress with little effort. I was merely at the 'bloated' stage of pregnancy, but my third pregnancy proved to be showing at a much faster rate than the previous ones. The top portion of my dress was covered in silver sequins that sparkled like diamonds when the light hit them just right, while the skirt, made from a chiffon material flowed gently with each movement of my leg. I felt and looked beautiful.

Kyle and I met up backstage and waited for the second dance team, married couple Bobby and Claire to finish their routines. They were rather impressive. Ms. Bolivar often complimented their form in class. While we may not have received the constant praise from our dance teacher, Kyle and I had worked very hard on our routines. I was proud of our progress.

"Maybe we should've practiced more." Kyle whispered to me, noticing their advanced skills.

I assured Kyle, while I adjusted his bow tie. "We're going to be fine, Kyle. We've worked very hard to get here. We should both be proud of our progress. Do you remember how bad we were at the beginning?" We were terrible.

When Bobby and Claire finished their routine, Ms. Bolivar took the microphone.

"Now our next couple are a dream team. They started as strangers, but finish as friends. Please welcome Kyle and Tilda with their favorite dance —The Waltz!"

"Here goes. Ready?" I said to Kyle before we made our debut.

"Ready." He took my hand to enter the stage.

We twirled and glided our way across the temporary stage. We met our counts and didn't step on a single toe. Kyle and I were so focused on our movements, we didn't realize the small stage ended before meeting our demise in mid-air.

Then…

We fell off the stage.

Shock and gasps were met in unison in the tiny "dance hall" that occupied all fifty of our supporters. To make matters worse, I landed on poor scrawny Kyle. Thankfully it was not a high stage. Our fall was only a few feet. Nevertheless, we went to an Urgent Care to make sure everything was fine.

"Well, Ma'am. Listening to the heartbeat, everything seems to be ok. I maybe would refrain from any further stage dancing though." The Urgent Care doctor advised. I think he was correct.

I let out a sigh of relief. "Thank you, doctor. I'll

take that advice into careful consideration."

Cassie, who anxiously drove me to the facility, came back with the kids and mouthed, "Are you okay?" Then let out a sigh of relief when I told her I was indeed perfectly fine.

We all walked out of the urgent care facility together, the kids on either side of me.

"I don't understand what happened. You guys were doing great and then suddenly 'whoosh' you were on the floor!" Cassie said.

"Well it sounds like the stage was extra slippery. I'm told Mr. and Mrs. Jones nearly had a similar fate prior to us. We just didn't see because we were prepping backstage." I felt happy they didn't fall of the stage because given their 75 years in age, somebody would be missing a fully functioning hip.

Livia took my hand. "Mama, are you sure you're not hurt? We'll take care of you tonight."

"Aww, you can definitely take care of me tonight, guys. I'm okay though. The doctor checked me out thoroughly." Thoroughly indeed. Because of my early pregnancy, the doctor had to use the alternate ultrasound procedure which included a wand going up my vagina. It was worth it, though, to know everything in there was safe and sound.

I wasn't feeling safe and sound emotionally, however. This fall made me realize I needed to talk to Deacon. But how? Between the time difference and playing phone tag, lately it was nearly impossible to talk. In fact, I hadn't heard from him for a couple of days.

Once the kids were asleep in bed, I crawled into a warm bath to ease my sore muscles and achy bones. I wasn't sure if the dancing or the fall made me feel worse. I wished I could listen to Deacon sing while I relaxed. I didn't think The Stag's Leap would be putting out any live CDs time soon, though. With his talent, he needed to be on a bigger stage, preferably one that wasn't so small and slippery that a person could slide off and possibly break a hip.

I woke up around 5:00 am to my doorbell ringing via my phone. I had finally invested in one of those fancy doorbells that captured video of would be intruders.

This intruder was a handsome 5'11" recently turned 29-year-old Irishman. I felt so excited, I flew out of bed, practically tripping on my sheets and falling again. Maybe it wasn't so much the stage's fault after all.

I clumsily unlocked the locks and flung open the door. There he stood, a couple of days scruff on his face. Bags under his eyes from flying all night. Wrinkled clothes from trying to sleep on an uncomfortable plane. He was still the finest looking man I had ever known.

He was here. With me. Almost as though he sensed I needed him more than ever.

"Deacon!" I cried, wrapping my arms around his tired body. He had two large suitcases with him which made me wonder if his stay was going to be longer. I couldn't even think about that now. I just needed to touch his bristly face. Brush my hands through his messy hair. Hug and kiss him with our, no doubt, wretched morning breath. I didn't care.

"I'm so sorry it took me so long. I've been traveling for days it seems like. I wanted to surprise you at your recital, but it didn't work out as planned. That's the unfortunate part of buying a cheap, last minute ticket."

Deacon walked through the door, setting his bags down next to the sofa. He picked me up and carried me up to my bedroom. We just snuggled together on the bed with his dirty clothes. Note to self, wash sheets later- airplane germs are the worst.

He held my hand to his heart.

"How did you know I needed you to be here?"

"I needed me to be here. This has been a rough couple of weeks. I needed you. Is everything okay with you?"

"Yes and no. Deacon, I have something I have to tell you."

He started to pale and looked extremely nervous. "Are you dumping me?"

"What? Oh my god no!"

"Phew. After flying from Dublin to Reykjavík, Reykjavik to Frankfurt, Frankfurt to New York, New York to here, that would've broken me, I'm afraid."

"Well, what I have to say might change your mind."

"Go on then."

"Okay, um, I'm just going to come out and say it. Shit, do you have any airplane booze? You might need it."

"Tilda, you're beginning to scare me. Is everything okay?"

"Deacon, I'm pregnant." I let a deep breath out. "Oh, and you're the father. I mean, obviously. I mean, I hope it's obvious."

He stared at me, motionless. I could see sweat form above his eyebrows.

"Did I break you?"

Suddenly, tears came to his eyes. He released a broad smile from his once frozen expression.

"Tilda, are you sure?"

"I'm positive. Literally. The urgent care doc confirmed it for me today."

"Wait. Why were you at the urgent care?" He exclaimed, feeling my stomach.

I completely forgot I hadn't told him about my disaster of a dance recital. I was glad he didn't surprise me then.

"Ugh, it was so embarrassing. Kyle and I fell off the stage."

"Holy shit! Are you okay?!"

"Yes, it was a small, low to the ground stage. I'm fine. That's why I went to the urgent care. Just to make sure."

Deacon didn't look convinced.

"I promise, we're okay, Deacon."

"Well what's wrong with Kyle? He couldn't save

you from falling off the goddamn stage?"

"Oh, don't blame Kyle. He feels bad enough. He doesn't even know I'm pregnant. He'd be devastated if he knew that." So far, besides me, there were only five people, six including George, who knew I was pregnant. I didn't plan on making Kyle the seventh anytime soon.

"Do you know how far along you are? I can't believe this. We've been so careful. Not that I'm not excited. I'm so excited, Tilda. This baby is exactly what I need. With my dad's passing, I've been so depressed and defeated."

"I'm pretty sure our spontaneous bathtub rendezvous is the cause of this." I pointed to my belly.

"Damn. You're fertile, Tilda Loxley. I'll keep that in mind for the future."

The future. What did the future hold? Besides a baby?

"Very funny. But we do need to discuss our future. How long will you be here?"

"My passport is stamped for six months. I have to go to the consulate for a Visa extension. That shouldn't be a problem as long as I don't let it lapse."

We laid back on the bed and Deacon held me.

"Please don't leave, Deacon."

"I don't plan on it, Tilda Loxley. Hmm. Tilda Kelly sounds quite good as well. But I'm not going to do that here."

"Ooh Deacon Kelly, is this a pre-proposal?!"

"Keep your knickers on. Or rather, let's not."

With that, he slid my 'knickers' off and showed me some new moves.

A short while later, we showered and got dressed, excited to surprise the kids on this lazy Sunday morning. They missed Deacon something awful.

"Kids! Wake up! I have a surprise." I called from downstairs.

Logan sluggishly walked out of his room and asked, "What's the surprise?"

"Mama, did you say surprise?" Livia asked, confused as she carefully came down the stairs.

Deacon walked through the door with a small box of fresh donuts. "How about some donuts!"

"Donuts!" Logan and Livia shouted together. "Deacon!!!!" They squealed immediately after that.

"Surprise! I come bearing gifts of sugar." He seemed as happy as they were, which warmed my heart. "You have to share some with us though."

"When did you get here??" Logan asked with a mouth full of a maple bar.

"Few hours ago. Are you surprised, Logan?"

"Yes!" My sweet son said, smiling.

"That was my plan. So, have you been taking good care of your mum while I've been gone?"

Logan dropped his head. "Yes. But she fell yesterday. But that wasn't our fault."

"Aww, baby, I know that wasn't your fault. Mommy is just clumsy. And I'm fine." Besides the lifetime of humiliation, all that remained from the fall was some bruises and an urgent care bill.

The kids went and played their Monopoly Junior board game while Deacon and I finished a cup of coffee on the sofa. It had to be one of the most content moments I'd experienced in a very long time.

Of course, that contentment was short lived.

"You have a text message, Tilda." Deacon passed me the phone.

How did the recital go? Did you win a gold trophy?

"Oh, it's just a text from Sam." I said, not thinking much about it, as I texted him back.

No trophy. I fell off the stage. But our counts were on point.

What???

"Who's Sam? I've never heard you mention her. A new friend?"

"Well, sort of. It's a funny story actually."

Deacon looked at me, waiting for my funny story. He wasn't a terribly possessive person in my experience. But would it be awkward explaining to him?

"I met Sam on our trip to the Northern Lights. Anyhoo, he was at the engagement party the other night. Turns out he is Kyle's fiancée Sarah's uncle. Funny right?"

You fell off the stage?? R U and baby okay??

"Why does he keep texting you?" Deacon seemed annoyed.

"I told him about what happened yesterday. He asked if the baby is okay."

I stopped in my tracks. Oh shit.

Deacon stopped fidgeting and stood up. "You told this random bloke, Sam, is it? You told him about you being pregnant before you even spoke to me about it?"

"Yes, but it's not like you think. We had coffee after, just as friends. And he figured it out. I couldn't eat the tiramisu, you see."

"Who paid?" Deacon asked, calmly.

Attempting to avoid the conversation I walked to the kitchen. I also wanted to get out of ear shot of the kids.

"What do you mean? Who paid for the tiramisu?"

"Who paid the bill, Tilda?" Deacon asked again, following me into the kitchen.

"Oh, well, I suppose Sam did."

He smiled, "That was a date, my love. Sam took you out on a coffee date."

"No. No it wasn't a date. I told him it wasn't."

"Just because you said it wasn't, I'm afraid Tilda, it was a date. He asked you out for coffee and paid for it."

Could it have been…a date… and Sam tricked me? Or could it have been just two new friends having coffee? I've paid for Cassie's coffee before. We are definitely not dating.

"I don't know Deacon. I think you're reading into things because you're a bit jealous."

"You bet I'm jealous. While I was traveling halfway across the world, some bloke was tricking my lady into a date."

"You make it sound like I am some inept woman who can't take care of herself. I resent that."

Deacon knew he was edging that line and about to go over it.

"I don't think that. I trust you, Tilda. Honestly, I do. I'm just tired and it's been a crazy morning. I'm not used to being in love. I'm sorry." He ran his hand through his thick, dark blonde hair, looking defeated.

"I'm sorry. I know you trust me. And it wasn't like that, you know, a date. I talked about you and he knows I'm with you."

I felt the need to at least text him back to let him know everything with the baby turned out fine. His repeat question mark texts were starting to annoy even me.

Yes. Minor fall. We're all okay. Deacon is here now to help. TTYL.

A thumbs up response let me know he understood and would finally stop texting me. While I did find him handsome, I had no feelings beyond friendship and wasn't really sure about that now Deacon was here. I can assure you, if he was having coffee with Shar Mahoney I'd be pissed. I resolved his aggravation and even jealousy was warranted.

Chapter 21

I had one last class for the Non-English speakers. After tonight, I knew with confidence, I could mark this Bucket List item off my list. I was going to miss the class that I'd gotten to know over the past several weeks.

I wouldn't have to miss Shira though. There was no way she would let me go. Somehow, I let it slip to her that I was pregnant, and she thus assured me I would receive Shira Check-Ins from time to time. She was busy herself with real school although considering her energy level, I wasn't concerned.

"I guess we'll go ahead and start class now. Is everything okay with Omar? He's usually the first one here."

"Omar got deported."

"What? That's terrible! What happened?"

Shira went on to explain that while Omar told the Turkish and United States government he came here to study at the local university, he had yet to attend a class. In fact, he wasn't even enrolled. The Turkish government found out and requested his passport and immediate return to Turkey.

I couldn't help but wonder how Shira knew all of this. I didn't think she would have called the authorities on him due to her massive annoyance of his English skills. She had a potty mouth, but I didn't feel like Shira was evil in any way.

Poor Omar. I didn't know him on a close personal level. He seemed like a nice, patient guy though. Anybody that has Shira yelling in your ear as much as she did without smacking her in the face must have the patience of Job.

We did a quick final lesson and I passed out the certificates that were mostly ceremonial but deserved. Since it was our last class, I invited everyone to bring their favorite dish from their home country for a potluck.

We had some spring rolls and noodles from JoJo, my Chinese student. Manuel, one of the students from Central America brought chicken tamales and a beans and rice dish. Shira brought hummus, flat bread and tabbouleh. She also brought baked chicken wings, which I wasn't sure was technically Israeli, but what Shira wants, Shira gets. She must have been craving actual food, instead of sad salads. Okay, I'm just being snarky Her salads are good. I just wish I could be skinny like Shira when I ate them.

That definitely was not happening anytime soon.

When I arrived back at the house, the kids were drawing and finishing up homework. Deacon was doing dishes in the kitchen and cleaning up from their dinner. Well, their dinner was courtesy of UberEATS but still, there was cleanup from the day.

I know all of those Instagram ladies brag about

how sexy their husbands are when they're doing housework, but it is kind of hot. Deacon had a kitchen towel draped over his shoulder as he unloaded the dishwasher. He didn't tend to wear jeans a lot, but instead opted for slacks that fit his derriere just perfectly, paired with a white shirt.

"Well this is a nice surprise. Maddie is a good babysitter, although she doesn't do dishes. I think I'll keep you around Mr. Kelly." I said, patting his cute behind.

There was no secret that I hated doing dishes. Well, I hated unloading dishes. It was such a tedious job that was never ending. At least cleaning them had some satisfaction. Putting away clean dishes just meant they were about to get dirty again.

None of that really mattered. I would do dishes happily every day if it meant Deacon was here with me.

"So, are you going to go work at Brodie's again?"

"What, I'm not earning my keep here? I guess I need to work a bit harder, eh?"

"That's not what I mean. I just don't want you to be bored."

He kissed me and said, "I don't think that's possible. But don't worry. I talked to my old boss and he's ready for me to come back and work. I left a guitar with Cassie so I can do my music as well. Apparently, the people have missed me." With an eyebrow raised, his crystal blue eyes twinkled as he smiled.

"Of course, they have darling. You're a star. You're my star but I must share you with the world. It's my social responsibility. That my dear, is how special you are. Although to be clear, I'm not sharing you with those women who come in to check out your butt when you're serving drinks. And you best be sure and throw away those phone numbers they leave for you at the end of the night."

He blushed in the cutest way. It was almost as though he didn't quite realize how desired he was. I acted like I was joking around with him, but it did make me uncomfortable. Deacon is a very friendly, charming person. He could flirt with the mailman and not even realize it. It's not like he wants to hop in bed with our mailman, he's just friendly that way.

As a woman for an appreciation of hot men, I was well aware how someone with that demeanor could provide signals in the wrong direction.

"So, when do you start back at the pub?" I asked, sitting down with the kids. My first trimester had made me incredibly tired. I also had yet to tell the kids, which was getting more and more difficult to put off.

"Mommy! Your stomach bounced." Livia exclaimed, shooting up in horror.

"Oh, I'm sorry. Maybe Mommy has gas."

Deacon burst into laughter at the idea that I farted out of my stomach. Livia didn't seem to find it convincing either.

"Tilda, might I have a word?" Deacon beckoned me from the kitchen. Livia thankfully was already distracted by something Logan was watching and forgot what happened.

"Sure, just a moment!" I said, forcing myself up. I still wasn't showing that much, but moving around was already difficult for me.

"Have you thought about what you're going to tell the kids? I mean, they're gonna figure it out soon."

"I know. I just don't know what to say."

He looked at me and smiled, gently brushing my hair back. "You could tell them we're in love. That we love each other and because of that, we're having a baby."

"Tell them we're in love? But what happens when they ask if we're getting married?! I'm supposed to say no, not right now. That's what people say when someone asks if they want some coffee. *No, not right now*."

"What's wrong with that? You aren't saying we won't ever."

"They're kids. What will their friends say? What is everyone going to say?" I started to feel the realization that I was 40 and pregnant with my young Irish boyfriend's baby. My body was going to change, I was going to get a lot bigger. I worked so hard to not get that way and all of that will be for naught.

"Tilda, you need to stop worrying about what people think and say. This is your life. Are you happy with me?"

"God yes." I had never been happier in fact. This 29-year-old man was more than anything I could have ever hoped for.

"Well that's good news. Me too. So, fuck them. Them outside, not the kids. The kids need to know the truth."

Deacon was right. I did need to include my children on one of the biggest surprises I've had in a very long time.

"Okay. Yes. I will tell them. I will, I mean, we will tell them tonight. Oh, and by the way, you never told me when you're starting back at Brodie's."

Deacon winced. "Actually, I'm supposed to be at the pub in a few minutes. I didn't want to leave in the middle of this conversation though."

"Are you serious? You were leaving for the night and just going to tell me now? Oh, I don't like where this is all going. I sound like a shrew. I need a minute."

"Look, it's going to be all right. You, I mean, we don't have to tell them tonight. We just need to tell them soon. How about after the ultrasound? I'm sorry Tilda. I have to go." I could tell he felt bad.

I got the kids ready for bed and took a look at Aunt Beebie's list. Her handwriting comforted me. Reading her letter over and over never got old. I wished she were here to counsel me. Tell me if I'm making the right decisions. Tell me if I'm not.

I only had one more thing on Aunt Beebie's bucket list to finish—the hot air balloon. I was just as nervous about that as the posing naked one. First of all, being up in high open air was not on my bucket list. Airplanes I could handle, standing in a basket and floating into the horizon, not so much. Secondly, how does one even find a hot air balloon person? What is a hot air balloon person even called?

I was nearing the "deadline" from my aunt, but I decided to put it on the backburner for a bit. This lady had a lot on her plate and one bun still in the oven...

Deacon and I agreed the best time to tell the kids would be after my first official, non-ER related ultrasound. My first appointment was scheduled for this morning, after the kids were off to school.

It was an odd feeling as we sat in the comfortable waiting room, equipped with an electric fireplace and plenty of maternity focused magazines. I hadn't done this visit in several years. Not to mention, it was with a completely different man. Deacon held my hand, perhaps to ease his own nerves as we waited patiently for the nurse to call out my name.

When I was pregnant with Logan, Steve came with me to nearly all my appointments. We were two young and eager first timers. When I got pregnant with Livia a few years later, the dynamic had changed a bit. His schedule was busier, we were busier with already having one child. I was difficult to be around since I never dealt with my first round of post-partem depression and anxiety.

Needless to say, I went to most of my doctor visits alone or with a young Logan.

A nurse opened the door and called my name to come back to the patient rooms.

"So how does this work? They just bring out the machine like on television and it shows the baby in there?" Deacon nervously asked as the nurse walked us to the room.

"Yep!" The bouncy nurse answered for me. "In fact, we have a special room just for ultrasounds. Is this your first time around?" She asked Deacon, who now began to perspire a bit above his brow.

"Yeah, it's that obvious?" He asked with a slight blush to the cheeks.

"It's okay. New dads are the best. They're so excited. You'll be fine." She patted him on the back as she handed me the infamous dressing gown. "You can keep your pants on. Just put this on the top, open in the front. I'll let Dr. Shah know you're here."

I awkwardly removed the top portion of my clothes and put the paper gown on.

"Knock knock." Dr. Shah poked her head in as I sat on the examination table. I was beginning to get a touch of the nerves as well. "I'm Dr. Shah. It's nice to meet you both."

The doctor pulled out her jelly, rubbed it all over my belly and then got to work.

"Well that was quick. Already found a heartbeat!" She moved across my belly, watching the screen, when she suddenly said, "Hmm."

"Hmm? What's hmmm?" I asked, since vagueness is not what one wants to hear during a medical exam.

She ignored me and just said, "Uh huh. Right then. Tilda, you have a perfectly healthy looking and sounding baby in there. To be clear, you also have another perfectly healthy and looking sounding baby in there. You guys are having twins."

Deacon coughed, cried and hyperventilated all in one moment. I just sat there in shock.

"Am I too old to have twins? Are you sure? Maybe the baby just moved around, and you found it again." I was definitely too old for twins. I was already too tired for one baby, but given this was partly my fault, I'd take one for our team. But now they were outnumbering me.

"Absolutely not, are you too old for twins. You're quite healthy. Sir, do you need a cup of water?" Dr. Shah turned her attention to Deacon, who still had not recovered from his cough, cry and hyperventilation experience.

"Yes, doctor. Could you have someone bring him some water." I asked.

"I'll be right back."

When Dr. Shah left the room, I turned to Deacon, "Are you having second thoughts about all of this? Deacon, are you okay? Please don't tell me you're having second thoughts because I can't get out of this. I'm in it for the long haul. I have two babies in here and they're just going to get bigger and bigger and..."

I rambled on forever until Deacon held my face, looked at me with tears in his eyes and kissed me with so much passion I thought I might pass out.

The doctor entered the room with the small bottle of water. “Oh, um, it seems you’re okay now. Wonderful.” She handed Deacon his water. “It’s okay, Dad. This is a common reaction to babies in general, not just twins. You’ll be fine.”

She handed Deacon a bag with a packet of information about anything and everything pre-natal. I got dressed, unsuccessfully trying to wipe off all remnants of the petroleum jelly from my stomach.

Deacon dropped me off at the house, then left to run an errand. He’d been quiet the entire ride home from the OB/GYN’s office.

I hoped he wasn’t hopping on a plane back to Ireland.

Chapter 22

I was happy to learn Deacon had not left me for a pint in Dublin. He returned home with a bouquet of beautiful flowers and a small cappuccino for me. I found him so handsome with his newsboy cap, dark slacks and white shirt. Some days I couldn't believe I was with such a fine-looking fella.

"I hope you don't mind. I called my mum with the news. She's over the moon with excitement."

"No, of course I don't mind." I said, sipping my first and probably only coffee of the day. "So that's why you were gone so long. I thought you'd taken off for Dublin." I joked.

"As if, Tilda Loxley. Not even twins could scare me away." He rubbed my belly. "Care to go upstairs with me? I'm finding you incredibly sexy right now."

"Are you serious? How can this be sexy? I'm a bloated mess."

"You are the mother of my children. Nothing sexier than that." Deacon ran his hand up my baggy sweater as he gently kissed my stomach. I hoped he knew life wouldn't be so spontaneous after the twins.

When the kids got home from school they played for a bit, then did their homework. I decided to order celebratory pizza for the upcoming announcement.

"So, Deacon and I have some exciting news. We

went to a doctor this morning and she gave us these pictures." I held out the photos from our ultrasound. "We're going to have two babies in the Spring, you guys!"

"What?! Two babies??" Livia exclaimed.

"Wow." Logan commented with shock.

"Are you guys going to get married?" Livia asked. That kid gets straight to the point.

Deacon cleared his throat, "I'm sure that's in the plan. Right now, we're just focusing on you guys and the babies. Is that okay with you?"

The kids looked at each other and shrugged, "Yeah that's fine. Can we eat our pizza now?"

Deacon laughed while he pulled out the plates from the cupboard. Logan and Livia eagerly waited for Deacon to hand them their pizza and breadsticks.

I whispered to Deacon, "Well I guess that went better than anticipated. They don't really seem fazed at all."

Deacon whispered back, "I think ordering the pizza was a smart call. You're the official decision maker in this relationship."

I poked him. "Oh no buddy. This is 60/40. You have to make decisions as well."

"60/40 huh? Not 50/50?"

"Well somebody has to be the boss. That'll be me."

"Perfect. Now, I hate to run off, but I have some money to make if I'm going to be a father of now, four children."

I melted. “You think of Logan and Liv as your children?”

He looked at me incredulously. “Of course, I do! What kind of guy do you think I am? I love your kids. Our kids. I hope you don’t mind. I don’t want to step on any toes. I know they had a dad.”

“They did and they’ll always have him in their hearts. I love you Deacon Kelly.”

“Love you too, Tilda Loxley. I’ll see you tonight.” With that, he kissed me and headed out to flirt with women to make excellent tips.

The next day I had a coffee date with Cassie. I had yet to break the news to her that I was officially pregnant with twins.

“Wow Tilda. When you go in, you go all in. How’s Deacon taking it. This must be awfully overwhelming for him.”

“He seems to be taking it fine. I mean, he nearly passed out at the doctor’s office but once it all set in, he was fine. I think? Enough about me, how are you doing? Is this divorce really happening?”

“Oh, it’s happening. He threw a bombshell on me last night though. It has recently come to his attention that he’s gay. Or at least feels attracted to men, I don’t know. It explains a lot though.”

Cassie looked to be on the verge of tears. I didn’t have the heart to tell her about the conversation I had with Deacon about it all.

“Wow. So, things are amicable?”

“Yes, I guess. I mean, I still feel all the feelings. Hurt, betrayal, insecurity, rejection and all that. I mean, our marriage was a lie sort of. But he has always been good to me and he loves the boys more than life itself."

"I'm sorry, Cassie. Why can't we be happy at the same time?"

"I guess life just doesn't work out that way."

"When you start dating again, I might have a guy for you. His name is Sam. I met him on our Northern Lights trip, and then would you believe I saw him again at the engagement party I went to?"

"Yuck. I have no interest in dating right now. I might even let myself eat whatever I want and gain ten pounds. Today."

"Trust me, you don't want to do that. Putting it on is a lot easier than taking it off. When my husband died, I ate my age in pounds of grilled cheese sandwiches."

"I'll keep that in my mind. In the meantime, I'm going to enjoy this almond croissant. It's delightful. How did you find this place?"

"That friend I was telling you about. His name is Sam. We came here after the party for coffee and dessert."

"Wait, you came here for a coffee date?"

"No, it wasn't a date. You sound just like Deacon. Just because he paid, it wasn't a date."

"Um, okay." Cassie said, pouring some raw sugar into her second latte.

And as though the man had heard his name being spoken, Sam walked in and got in line to order something.

"Holy shit. He must be a wizard or something."

"Who?"

"Sam. He's here! Right now!"

"What?! Where? I want to see what he looks like. For future reference only."

He must not be a wizard and simply a frequent customer because I heard the baristas say, "Hi Sam," when he walked up to order his drink.

He did, however, notice us gawking, because once he got his coffee and bagel, he walked over to us. "Well this is a surprise! How are you doing, Tilda?"

"I'm great. Still pregnant. Twins, it turns out. Sam, this is my best friend Cassie. Cassie this is Sam. Cassie is currently going through a divorce and has two boys. Sam is already divorced with a son in Chicago. He travels a lot. Sam, not the boy."

They both looked shocked at my rather thorough introduction.

"What? You're both attractive and single. Cassie, you know since your husband is gay that you aren't getting back together. Sam, you need a lady to help keep you grounded since you travel so much."

"Um Tilda, as much as I appreciate your assistance, I don't think Sam and I need to be fixed up at the moment." Cassie said, red faced with either embarrassment or fury.

"I'm sorry you guys. I have all this weird energy right now." Once I realized what I had said to Sam and Cassie, I felt terribly embarrassed, for myself and them.

"Apology not needed, Tilda. Cassie, it is wonderful to meet you. I'm off to the gym and then the airport. Tilda's right, I do travel a lot."

Sam said his goodbyes and headed out.

"Oh my god, Tilda. He's beautiful. Are you sure you don't want to date him?"

"What?! No! But you should."

"I don't think he's interested. But I'll keep him in my mind. That smile…and those teeth. And how is he so tan?"

"I think it's probably from the places he goes. He's a travel photographer."

"Well, once I'm back on my feet, socially, we'll check back with him. Okay?"

I smiled with childish excitement. "Yes!"

"Oh, and what do you want to do for your birthday? It's coming up and I didn't forget this year."

"Honestly, Cass, I don't want to do anything special. I just want to order in some food, eat some pie and watch a good show on one of the twenty different streaming services I've subscribed to."

"Are you sure?"

"Definitely. I don't want to do a thing."

"Okay. Does Deacon know that?"

"I don't know why?"

"Just wondering. It's your first birthday as an official couple. I just thought he might have something planned."

"We've been so busy with everything I don't think he's planning anything."

"Ah so the honeymoon is over?"
"No, but yes. I guess it is."

Chapter 23

It was October. My birthday had arrived, although I didn't feel terribly excited about it. I was 41, nearly 12 weeks pregnant with twins, twenty-five pounds heavier than last year and not glowing.

But I had two amazing kids, two darling babies on the way and an incredible partner. When I told Deacon, I didn't want to do anything, he was fine with that. I was feeling kind of depressed because my year was ending, and I hadn't finished Aunt Beebie's bucket list.

There was no way this pregnant lady was getting into a hot air balloon anytime soon.

Deacon ordered my Thai food for lunch, picked up my four different slices of pie because I couldn't choose which one, and set up my favorite show on Amazon Prime to watch in peace and quiet with my new sound-proof headphones.

It was a Saturday, which meant Deacon had to work since that was the busiest night of the week at Brodie's. He could pull in triple digit tips, which goes pretty far towards buying new baby gear. I continued to tell him I had plenty of money to provide for us. Deacon insisted however that he contribute monetarily to our family. I didn't argue because I knew it was important to him.

"Tilda, there is just one thing I wanted to do before I leave for work later. Are up for a ride with me? The kids are still at Cassie's for their playdate. We can pick them up on the way back home."

"Oh, I don't know Deacon. I'm only three episodes into the new season of Marvelous Mrs. Maisel. Can you just go alone?"

"Well, since I'm working tonight, I thought it would be nice to spend as much time as I could with you."

That made me feel bad, so I put on more suitable clothes, brushed my teeth and slapped some tinted moisturizer on. Just in case we saw anybody I knew. I probably needed a break from television anyway. I was missing Aunt Beebie extra today, so I put on my necklace with her ashes in it.

"Where are we going?" I asked as I carefully got into his car.

"I just have an errand to run. I grabbed a coat for you just in case it gets chilly in the air, I mean outside."

We pulled into the parking lot of our local supermarket. Nearby, there was a van with the sticker, "Al's Balloon Adventures" along the side.

Deacon waved to the guy, who seemed to recognize him.

"Deacon, what's going on?" I asked, suspiciously.

"Don't be mad Tilda, but I knew you were depressed about not finishing your bucket list. So, I did some Google searches, called these guys and set up a private hot air balloon ride for us." He said, matter of fact.

"This should be good. How on earth will I be able

to climb into a hot air balloon basket?"

"Well ma'am, it's called a gondola and we'll help you in."

"Did you tell him I'm pregnant?" I whispered to Deacon as we got into the van. "Do we know if he's not a serial killer?"

"Yes, he came recommended by some customers at the pub. Tilda, not everyone is a serial killer."

"I know but you just never know. We got into a van with a complete stranger. He could have easily slapped that sticker on the side, and we'd be none the wiser."

The van driver, who probably overheard our entire conversation added, "We'll be at the field in a few minutes. Are you ready for an exciting time?"

"No, not really. I'm afraid of heights."

"Ah, once you see the view and feel the relaxing movement as you float across the sky it will make you forget your fears."

I hoped he was right. I wondered if Aunt Beebie was afraid of heights. Most of her bucket list items were about conquering fears. My fears anyway. I got through being naked in front of strangers, singing to an audience, learning to dance. I even kissed a stranger with reckless abandon. That turned out quite well. And now, I was about step into a hot air balloon and sail across the sky. Major fear conquering.

We walked through the grassy field to the hot air balloon where a couple with Al's team were setting up the balloon. I took some deep breaths to calm my nerves.

"I hope you're okay with this. I didn't mean to scare you. I wanted to help you finish your list."

"Oh Deacon, I'm terrified. But it's fine. I needed this push. Aunt Beebie would be enthralled with you, I think." I rubbed my necklace, feeling her in my heart. Wishing she could give me some extra confidence.

"All right, folks! I think we're ready." The man motioned us over to the gondola. Deacon had to help me in because moving around wasn't quite as easy as it once was.

"I'm sure the doctor would be super happy to hear I'm doing this." I said, sarcastically.

"It's fine. I called her to double check." Deacon said, not missing a beat.

He put his arms around me as the burner shot out a loud noise and the balloon rose up. We brushed against some trees, which the crew assured me was perfectly normal and not going to rip the basket or balloon.

We rose higher and higher, to the point where nearby towns seemed small. Deacon, with his arms still around my shoulders, turned to me. His beautiful blue eyes smiling. He seemed a bit nervous, which I wasn't familiar with because Deacon Kelly is one of the most confident people I knew.

He bent down on one knee and looked up at me.

"Tilda Loxley, we started this adventure nearly a year ago to the day. Tonight, you're ending this adventure but if you'll have me, I'd love it if you'd start a new one with me. I love you, Tilda with all my heart. Will you marry me?"

Everyone in the hot air balloon had stopped everything. It was completely silent, with the exception of the hot air balloon burner roaring above. Regardless, it was still the most romantic moment I'd ever had in my entire life. I wanted to pass out with joy. I felt like I could pass out with joy.

"Deacon Kelly, of course I'll marry you."

We pretty much kissed the whole rest of the balloon ride and missed a good bit of the view, but I didn't mind. Aunt Beebie would have been elated if she were here. In a way, she was.

When the balloon landed, Cassie was at our location with the kids. A small table was set up with champagne.

"Deacon, I can't drink this." I said, somewhat disappointed.

"Yes, you can. It's sparkling white grape juice." He winked at me as he handed me the champagne flute of juice. He really thought of everything.

Cassie, who was aware of this plan the entire time cried tears of joy and hugged me. The kids, who were also in on the plan cheered. How Deacon was able to keep them from telling me was beyond me.

"Tilda, I am so happy for you. We're going to be related now!" Cassie nudged me as we watched Deacon pour "champagne" for the kids.

Livia didn't enjoy the sparkling juice, judging by her face. But Logan seemed to. Livia still had time to become more adventurous. I mean, look at me. It took me 40 years to live up to my potential.

All because of Aunt Beebie's Bucket List.

Epilogue

My favorite season has always been autumn. The sound of crumpling leaves, smoke escaping from the chimneys of nearby homes, pumpkin bread. I haven't had much time for baking pumpkin bread, however. My life has taken a far busier turn.

"Mommy, when do Michael and Jameson get here? I've been waiting forever!" Livia said, staring out the window. Every huff and puff left fog lingering on the glass. Although Livia could be somewhat dramatic, I agreed that forever was accurate. I hadn't seen my best friend Cassie for five months. She came to visit me for a week during my wedding in June, which was wonderful. However, life is so busy, neither of us could just get up and leave at a moment's desire to visit one another. Thank goodness for modern technology to keep up with everyone's life, and to simply check in and see a familiar face.

"Liv, they won't be here for another couple of hours. How about we go check on Deacon at the pub, B & B are just waking up. They'll be ready for an adventure." These days, adventures are simply short walks to the pub, park and corner supermarket.

"Can we have a Coke while we're there?" Logan asked.

"No, I told you numerous times. One soda a week. You had it already!" In fact, I may have lost count and already allowed his next week soda this week. I have four kids now to keep track of on half the sleep. The struggle is most definitely real.

I bundled up the twins while Logan and Livia put on their coats and rain boots to walk down to the pub. At the door I said, "Take care of the house, George while we're out. We won't be gone long." George, who was busy napping on the sofa, lifted her head in acknowledgement, then went back to her afternoon siesta.

Our house is a quick walk to The Stag's Leap, which is quite convenient. The large two-story home was once a vacation rental, our previous rental in fact. I fell in love with it then and when Deacon and I made the decision to make Ireland our new home, I knew this was the house I wanted. A fair offer, well... perhaps a little more than fair, and it was ours. It needed some updating to be sure but soon it would be the home of my Pinterest dreams.

When we arrived at the cozy Stag's Leap, we settled at our spot by the fireplace. It has ample room for our portable crib and stroller. It's also near the bar so we can chat with Deacon. Now that Deacon was a nervous parent, the once free and open fireplace had been set up with all sorts of safety precautions. It now had a secure cover and no more pokers or pieces of wood sitting nearby for children to poke an eye out with. While it was bittersweet because Deacon's father, James had passed away, Deacon thrived as the new landlord. I knew James would be proud of his son.

"Well hello my loves! What brings you in? I thought you were waiting for Cassie to come before you came down?" Deacon came out from behind the bar to greet us, with his towel on one shoulder, apron around his waist and smile that could kill. His smile still gave me goosebumps. Even on four hours of sleep.

"We're bored." Livia announced, running over to the bar for a bag of crisps. I followed to grab the kids some waters from the small refrigerator behind the bar.

"Deacon, can I have a Coke?" Logan whispered to Deacon, while helping him move the twins from their stroller into their portable crib.

Deacon, who also can't keep track of Logan's soda consumption, simply looked at me.

"No, Deacon. He can't have a Coke. Honestly, Logan. Nice try." I took Logan's coat and handed him the bottle of water.

It was the middle of the day and somewhat busy because it was a football Saturday. The regulars typically came in to watch the match and have lunch and a beer. Our busiest day was always Sunday though because we had a wonderful Sunday dinner on the menu. As it turned out, when Deacon's brother-in-law, Donno, wasn't busting up noses and drinking beer, he was a phenomenal cook. Each Sunday we served prime rib alongside Yorkshire Pudding, roasted root vegetables and parmesan crusted mashed potatoes cooked to perfection. I've gained five pounds since I've moved to Ireland.

"Mama, you have a text from Aunt Cassie." Logan said, picking up his baby sister, who was protesting her confined space.

"She's on her way! The flight came in early!" I was so excited to see her I thought I would cry. Deacon's family has been wonderful. I've become quite close with his sister, Orla, and even his mother, Mary. But nobody could replace Cassie.

I quickly texted her back, letting her know to meet us at the pub, I had a special table reserved for her and the kids.

Since Saturday is a busy day, I typically help Deacon and Doris by taking table orders and delivering drinks. The pub is an open space filled with tables where I'm able to see the kids and work at the same time, helping Logan if he needs it. He has become a vital help now that the twins were here. Keeping busy also helped me pass the time until my best friend finally arrived. It didn't take long, however.

I felt the cold rush in when the door opened. Then I heard a loud squeal echo through the room.

"Tilda!!! Happy Thanksgiving!!" Cassie ran in, dragging her bags along with her. Michael and Jameson ran straight to Logan and Livia with as much excitement as Cassie. While we didn't technically celebrate Thanksgiving in Ireland, Cassie and I still planned on observing our American holiday on Thursday. It was also the perfect opportunity for her to visit while her kids had a week off school.

Logan and Livia's grandparents were also coming to visit for the Thanksgiving celebration. Their plane was scheduled to arrive on Monday. We have gotten closer since the twins were born and I got married again. They were very supportive of our move to Ireland, which surprised me, but also lifted a great weight off my shoulders.

Cassie squirmed. "I know it's a full house with Logan and Livia's grandparents coming. I hope you don't mind another guest, because I brought a friend with us."

"A friend? Who?" I couldn't imagine Tabitha would've come all this way on a whim. I spoke with her the other day and she was busy with her new personal trainer You Tube video productions. It's a whole thing apparently.

"He's just finishing up with the taxi driver."

"He?"

When the door opened again, I heard a familiar man's voice say, "Well hello Tilda! Fancy seeing you here!" It was Sam. Sam from the Northern Lights trip!

"Cassie, you did not tell me you were seeing Sam!"

"Well, I met up with him at that coffee place with the good desserts a few times after you moved, and it just seemed to work. We started seeing each other more often and it turned into something more than that. I wanted to wait to tell you until I knew I really liked him…and I do."

Cassie and Sam exchanged looks with a slight blush to their cheeks.

I caught Deacon, who returned back from pouring and dropping off drinks.

"Deacon, wait, I haven't introduced you. Sam, this is my husband, Deacon. Deacon this is Sam. He's my friend from our Northern Lights trip!" I could see Deacon realize this was the same guy he was somewhat jealous about a long time ago. Clearly, he had nothing to worry about because Sam and Cassie appeared smitten with one another.

Deacon extended his hand to shake and asked, "Sam, why don't we go get you a drink. Are you a Guinness man?"

"Why yes, I am."

"Good answer. Guinness is our nectar of the gods. Come on. I'll introduce you to the fellas watching the match."

Sam and Deacon walked over to the bar while Cassie and I caught up with the kids at our side.

"Tilda, your precious Beebies! They've gotten so big!" Cassie said, excitedly.

"They turned seven months last week. Brennan and Brianna say hi to your Aunt Cassie!" Cassie was technically a cousin, but the age difference was so big, we decided she could be an aunt. I didn't have a sister by blood and Cassie was the closest to one I've ever had.

She picked up Brennan. "They are absolute perfection, Tilda. You really have it all. Finally. I am so happy for you."

"Thanks. I've never been happier. Logan and Livia have settled in better than I expected. The twins are doing wonderful and I spend a lot of time in a pub and sleep with the guitar player. How could things get any better?"

"I have a few ideas." Sam said as he approached our table.

"Oh, Tilda, I haven't had a chance to tell you. Sam and I want to start a travel company, specifically for American tourists coming to Ireland. He has so much experience and this way he wouldn't have to travel so much. We'd base it here and in Chicago so he can see his son frequently. I'd move here with the boys. What do you think?"

"Are you serious? I think that's amazing!" I was so elated I practically fell off my chair. "But what does Erik think about it? Moving the kids so far away."

"Well, he wasn't excited about it at first. But he recognizes that he works a lot and can work out times to come visit us. I have a lot of family here. It would be nice for the kids to get to know them."

Deacon came over to our table with a tray of drinks for everyone. "I've heard some congratulations are in order! Have you guys set a date yet?"

I looked at Cassie, confused.

"Oh yes, and one more thing, Sam proposed to me last night. We're getting married!"

Deacon drew me closer to his side and kissed me on the cheek. We had a wedding to help plan, four amazing kids and my best friend would be moving her family to Ireland—with me! I had a feeling life was about to take a new adventurous turn.

ACKNOWLEDGEMENTS

Writing a book is not an easy task and I would not be able to do it without the help and support from a lot of people.

I would like to thank my husband Paul and my two fabulous kids for being patient and understanding. You guys are the best and I am the luckiest gal in the world. I would also like to thank my dog Charlie and cat Jennie for keeping me company in the office while I write.

I have a huge shout out to Marla, my editor who works tirelessly to help perfect what I write. You push me to be a better writer without completely crippling my soul. I appreciate your honesty, candor but mostly your kindness. Thank you.

Thank you to Marti, who spent hours at her computer helping me with cover design issues. I'm proud to call you my sister from another mister.

Many thanks to Louise for telling me about her life changing trip to see Aurora Borealis. It was like I was there.

Finally, I would like to thank from the bottom of my heart, all my friends, family and strangers who have supported me on this journey. Your kind words, Facebook shares and feedback when I have questions about something are so appreciated. Cheers!

ABOUT THE AUTHOR

Leah Battaglio is the author of Disillusion Meets Delight, Cutthroat Confections and A Bucket List of Sorts. She lives in Mckinney, TX with her family and pets.

www.leahbattaglio.com

Printed in Great Britain
by Amazon